Critical Acclaim for Nina Bawden

'The success of this remarkably well-written novel is that it takes such an ordinary shell and uses it to reveal with skill and sympathy the nature of a rather neglected woman' – *Daily Telegraph*

'Miss Bawden, through her sensibility and the quality of her perception, teaches us to refrain from judging, which is one of the civilising and remedial elements in art. I really warm to Miss Bawden' – *Sunday Times*

'She tells quiet stories, quietly, devastatingly . . . few women novelists are writing better' – *Punch*

'With her usual marvellous economy of words and attention to detail, Nina Bawden unfolds for us a portrait of Elizabeth, verging on middle age at a domestic and sexual crossroads'
– *Books and Bookmen*

VIRAGO
MODERN
CLASSIC

NUMBER
366

NINA BAWDEN

was born in London in 1925 and evacuated to South Wales during the war. She was educated at Ilford County High School for Girls and at Somerville College, Oxford.

Her first novel, *Who Calls the Tune*, appeared in 1953. Since then she has published nineteen other adult novels including: *Tortoise by Candlelight* (1963); *A Little Love, A Little Learning* (1965); *A Woman of My Age* (1967); *The Birds on the Trees* (1970); *Walking Naked* (1981), all of which are published by Virago; *Afternoon of a Good Woman*, winner of the Yorkshire Post Novel of the Year Award for 1976 and *Circles of Deceit*, which was shortlisted for the Booker Prize in 1988 and has recently been filmed by the BBC. Her most recent novel is *Family Money* (1991, also published by Virago).

Nina Bawden is also an acclaimed author of sixteen children's books. Many of these have been televised or filmed; all have been widely translated. Amongst them are: *Carrie's War* (1973); *The Peppermint Pig*, the recipient of the 1975 Guardian Award for Children's Fiction; *The Finding* (1985), *Keeping Henry* (1988), *The Outside Child* (1989) and *Humbug* (1992).

For ten years Nina Bawden served as a magistrate, both in her local court and in the Crown Court. She also sat on the councils of various literary bodies, including the Royal Society of Literature – of which she is a Fellow – PEN, the Society of Authors, and the A.L.C.S., and is the President of the Society of Women Writers and Journalists. In addition she has lectured at conferences and universities, on Arts Council tours and in Schools.

Nina Bawden has been married twice and has one son, one daughter and two stepdaughters. She lives in London and in Greece.

For my father
Charles Mabey
on his eightieth birthday

Nina Bawden

A WOMAN
OF MY AGE

Published by VIRAGO PRESS Limited 1991
20–23 Mandela Street, Camden Town, London NW1 0HQ

Reprinted 1992

First published in Great Britain by Longman, Green & Co. Ltd. 1967
Copyright © Nina Bawden 1967

A CIP catalogue record for this book is available from the British Library

Printed in Great Britain by
Cox & Wyman Ltd., Reading, Berks.

Chapter One

Somewhere between Meknes and Fez, the bus came to a sudden halt. The driver shouted something and got out, slamming the door. No one else moved.

The Arabs, shrouded in their burnouses, sat with their eyes closed. Now there was no longer a breeze through the windows, the bus became very hot. There was total silence except for a fly that circled, buzzing; it settled on my knee and rubbed its back legs busily. I brushed it off; the small movement made Richard shift irritably beside me. Neither of us is fat, but we were cramped on the hard, narrow seat and our clothes were too tight. My brassiere strap cut into my shoulders; Richard's belly bulged over his belt. The Arabs, in their voluminous garments, seemed much more comfortable. Perched together in pairs, they looked like white, roosting birds.

The image remains. But it is all. For most of the time other people are under-developed negatives, snapshots taken at different times and in different poses. You know other people only as witnesses to your own situation: when they reflect your own fears and desires, obstruct or extend them.

When does this happen? At what point, for example, did the Hobbs become real, develop in my mind like photographs coming to life in an acid tank? There may have been a moment on the boat to Tangier, perhaps, when they sat at our table in the tilting saloon and Mrs Hobbs talked about her bungalow in Kent – *my* bungalow, she said, *my* roses, while her husband smiled, content, apparently, to be a man without possessions – but if there was, I cannot remember it. On the road to Fez, several days after that brief sea voyage, I may have thought of them once or twice but I had no sense of their continuing existence. They had been fellow travellers, that was all, no more to me than the roosting Arabs in that bus.

Richard says I 'encouraged' them – he has his mother's lace-curtain mind. Nonni disapproves of the people who drop into the house at all hours and sit in our kitchen, drinking gin: both she and Richard believe guests should be carefully selected, come at stated hours and always wipe their feet. No – Richard is nicer than that. He simply believes it is unfair to be over-amiable to people you are not interested in. And excessive amiability is one of my faults, he tells me. It is a kind of laziness.

Perhaps it is a fault, though he is wrong about the laziness. If I was pleasant to the Hobbs on the boat, I was deferring to that third person *reportage* that runs constantly in my mind. *Elizabeth is such a nice person, she puts herself out for the most boring people.*

This inner voice is sometimes a moral arbiter of action, sometimes a high-toned excuser, but more often a way of giving myself some kind of shape. Of helping me to see myself.

I find this so difficult. When I look in the mirror – not to see if the grey roots are beginning to show before the next tinting, but in the same way I used to look at myself when I was seventeen, at *what*, *whom* and *why* – I remain, as I did then, cloudy, fading, sadly out of focus. I do not know myself, only my own situation: I am Elizabeth Jourdelay, married to Richard, the mother of his two sons. I am, *I am* middle-aged. This is an embarrassment that has come upon me suddenly, taking me by surprise so that I don't really believe it. Looking in the mirror I see the wrinkles, but perhaps tomorrow they will be gone and my skin will be smooth

8

again. Though wrinkles are not important. The important thing is that I am in the middle of my life and I feel as I did when I was adolescent, that I do not know where to go from here.

What of the time between? What have I done – *become* – during twenty long battling years? Is there no answer, no key?

Sitting in the hot, motionless bus, I am suddenly weighed down, heavy, inert and shapeless. An old woman, dull and futureless. And yet last night, when we were sitting in the restaurant in Meknes, the small lights twinkling (Richard said something about the electricity supply), the looking-glass on the near wall restoring some element of magic, of memory, we were young, tall, handsome. We talked and laughed and got drunk, showing off to each other like strangers.

This mood, that mood. Last night I was a young woman, well under thirty. Now I am an old one, feet aching, cheeks hanging in pouches, sodden with meaningless sadness.

'I told you we should have hired a car and not relied on the bus,' Richard said.

He told me, of course, nothing of the sort. We had planned all along to hire a car in Fez and drive over the Atlas, down to the desert. I looked at him. There was a line of black skin on his lips; he was pulling at it cautiously with his thumb and forefinger, wrinkling his nose. The skin of his nose is coarse, pitted with open pores. Sometimes he buys astringent lotion to dab on, as he buys things to rub into his scalp. Half empty bottles crowd our medicine chest, each a small epitaph: when I tidy them, they make me tender towards him.

I put out my hand. He took it and, after a second, handed it back to me like a borrowed handkerchief. He made a sound, a dry croak in his throat, and, because I was looking at him, straightened up, tightening his stomach muscles, lifting his chin. Once, he had a casual, Byronic look, dressed in velvet jackets and wore his dark hair long. Now his features have solidified and he looks like a Roman emperor.

9

Perhaps he will die, I thought. I closed my eyes and planned. I can move the boys into the spare room, they will be crowded but they will have to manage. Letting their rooms would bring in perhaps eight pounds a week. Moving out of my bedroom into the study, a little more. I will be able to get rid of Richard's desk which has always been an eyesore, a nasty, gimcrack affair he had as a boy, and put my bed against that wall. Nonni's room, which is on the ground floor and has its own bathroom would be a good one to let, but she cannot be moved upstairs because her stroke has left her paralysed on one side. She will be a major problem as I will have to get a full-time job and she needs looking after. But it would be unthinkable – that is, I must refuse to think of it – to send my crippled mother-in-law into a home, push her out of my life like some old, unwanted animal. . . .

Elizabeth is a heroine; she has done marvels; who would have thought she had such courage, such tenacity . . . ?

I laughed out loud, and Richard stared.

'I was thinking about the Hobbs.'

He looked unconvinced: Mr and Mrs Hobbs had not amused *him*. He looked at his watch. 'It's absurd, we've been here nearly half an hour,' he said, incredulous at this mean trick fate had played upon him and a little angry because he couldn't, rationally, blame me for it.

As if at some pre-arranged signal, the passengers rose and began to file out of the bus. They moved slowly, very patient and polite. A tall man in a sky-blue robe waited while Richard grovelled, his bottom sticking out into the aisle, for the precious canvas bag that held our travel documents and a half empty bottle of fizzy water. He looked at me gravely over my husband's bent back; his steady stare seemed somehow disapproving and I smiled at him because I prefer to be approved of. His thin, burned hand emerged from the folds of blue cloth and held out a small, lidless tin filled with yellow cough lozenges. I took one, thanked him, and put it quickly in my mouth before Richard could stand up. He is nervous of the food and drink abroad: in Meknes, he was angry because I brushed my teeth with water from the bathroom tap.

Outside the bus, everyone had settled on a patch of sparse grass at the side of the road. A stream ran beside it and a man was dabbling his child's feet in the water. She was a tiny girl with henna plastered on her hair and gold ear-rings; she laughed and drew up her feet. The rest of the passengers crouched patiently on their haunches; the women, who had removed their yashmaks in the bus, had now replaced them so that nothing could be seen of them but their eyes. Feeling the heat prickle on my bare arms and on the reddening skin of my neck, I realized that their clothes were more sensible than mine. The stream tinkled and made me thirsty; I went to stand beside it, watching the little girl, and wondering if I should bathe my feet.

'Bilharzia,' Richard said, though I had made no move to take my sandals off. He gave this warning with relish, liking to feel there were dangers lurking in this foreign land.

'I wasn't going to.'

'No?' He grinned. The sun made him look paler than usual, and younger.

'Well . . .'

We laughed together. Our feelings for each other rattle round like cards in a spinning tombola. Love, rage, dislike, tenderness – we draw out a card, not always appropriate, for each occasion.

The bus driver came to the side of the road and filled a battered tin with water. Richard spoke to him in French as he crouched by the stream wearing an old Army tunic over baggy, white trousers. He was so thin that he looked, in those oddly assorted garments, like a jointed scarecrow. I wondered if I should try to lose a little weight on this trip, just a cup of coffee for breakfast, a light lunch. Richard was talking rapidly, waving his hands in a Continental way. The driver laughed hilariously at something he said and walked back to the bus, a trail of water dripping from a hole in the bottom of the tin.

'There's a leak in the radiator,' Richard said. 'He says they'll get it going soon, though God knows – that bus must have been on the road since the year dot! I don't suppose there have been any spare parts brought into this country since the French left. I only hope our car doesn't break down in the desert.'

He looked cheerful at this adventurous prospect. We walked slowly out of the shade of the bus, up the long, straight road towards a clump of stunted trees. On either side the flat land stretched away, blue with heat and distance.

Richard said, 'It's surprisingly fertile here. Of course, it'll be different the other side of the Atlas.' He turned over a sod of dry earth with his toe, frowning like a farmer.

'Hotter, too.'

I longed for the desert. My life was crowded, cluttered up. I longed for broad, flat skies, wide horizons, emptiness. . . .

'Mr Hobbs has always wanted to see the desert,' his wife informed us. 'When he was a little boy, he wanted to join the Foreign Legion.'

She told us so much in so short a time – about her three grown-up sons, the colour of the curtains in her lounge and how they had had such trouble matching the blue in the Indian carpet, what kind of television set she had and which were her favourite programmes, what she thought of foreign food and how she made apple charlotte, baking wholemeal breadcrumbs overnight in the Aga cooker with which she had recently replaced her electric stove – pouring it all out in a haemorrhage of information, so it is hard to remember exactly when she told us this.

I think it must have been that afternoon when they picked us up in their chauffeur-driven car, sweeping by in a cloud of dusty air and stopping a few yards further on with a squeal of brakes. 'This must be Samaria, after all,' Richard said, as we removed our suitcases from the stranded bus.

Certainly, I have a clear visual memory of her, bouncing on the seat as the car lurched over a rut in the road and smiling indulgently – *all men are little boys at heart*. Her face was unlined and apple-shiny as a child's and her eyes naïve and clear, a washed, bright blue.

Her husband's eyes were cool, sea-grey, and perpetually wrinkled at the corners, either from nervousness, or at some private joke. Perhaps inner amusement was an habitual defence against his wife's garrulousness. He was narrowly built, an elegantly elongated man with a long, caved-in face and long, narrow hands that had pale cuticle moons on the finger-nails. He reminded me, for no reason I could pin down, of a stone crusader on a tomb.

He had reddened slightly at his wife's disclosure: perhaps his boyhood's dream was still precious to him. He said, with an apologetic, preliminary cough, 'I thought Morocco would make a change from Bournemouth.'

Mrs Hobbs sighed. 'We always go to the same hotel. They know us there and we always have the same room, facing the sea, you know, but nice and high up, so it's quiet at night.'

I said, 'It'll be very hot in the desert. Won't that bother you?'

She was so helplessly fat. Her breasts were pushed up by her corset into a single, jutting prominence; her thighs fell apart as she sat because her muscles could no longer hold them in any other position. And like many fat women, she had little, fluttery hands which she lifted and let fall in small, meaningless gestures, like birds blown on a current of air. My question was not impertinent: she had told us, on the boat, that she had a heart condition and had to be careful.

'Oh, I shall manage,' she said, and raised her left hand as if to fan herself, but the effort was too much and it dropped into her lap, resting there, small and white like a seagull on the billows. 'I want Mr Hobbs to have a good holiday,' she said. 'Once he retires, we shall have to draw our horns in.'

Retires from what? I may have wondered, but if I did it was only idly, too idly to ask. I was grateful to the Hobbs for

13

this rescue operation but I could not summon up any real interest in them, nor see any reason why I should try. They were a dull pair, kind and genuine enough, but totally predictable. Or so, it seemed. I know that if anyone had told me, that afternoon, how we were to become so terribly involved with them, it would have seemed incredible to me. (There are days when it still seems incredible, even now.)

Whatever Mr Hobbs's career, it had obviously always been subordinated to his wife's nesting instincts. She addressed him as 'Daddy'. 'Didn't we, Daddy?' Or, 'Isn't that right, Daddy?' Thus appealed to, he murmured something appropriate and smiled, though it seemed with some discomfort. Then, suddenly, she said, 'Oh, I *am* sorry, dear,' and clapped her little hand across her mouth. She looked at me with her innocent, child's eyes—her age and weight seemed ludicrous when you looked at her eyes: it was as if someone had taken a young and pretty girl, blown her up with a pump and dressed her, for some freakish purpose, in a hideously old-fashioned silk dress and elastic stockings. 'Do you know,' she said, 'I promised him before we started out that I *would* try not to call him Daddy. It's so difficult, though, you get into the habit, you know how it is.'

'But no one likes to be thought of purely in terms of their biological function,' Mr Hobbs said.

Richard and I laughed, and he seemed shyly grateful: perhaps he had often thought of this mild little joke and never hoped to have a chance to make it. It was so exactly the kind of pleasure I have sometimes known myself that I felt, all at once, a kind of intimacy with him.

Besides, what am I except a wife and mother? Who thinks of *me* in any other terms?

Chapter Two

'Of course, if you get married now,' Aunt Lilian said, 'you may not find it so easy to get into politics.'

'You mean because Richard isn't interested?'

Aunt Lilian hesitated. 'Naturally, it would make a difference. He will want you at home, not always running about to meetings.'

'One must look ahead.' Aunt Kit stubbed out her cigarette. She smoked continuously, even when she gave music lessons: her broad, pianist's fingers and the white hairs of her moustache were stained a yellowy brown. 'How would he feel, for example, if you became a Member of Parliament?'

Since I was twenty years old and had had some success in college debating societies, this possibility did not strike me as remote. Nor did it seem so to my aunts. They were used to taking the young seriously, and they were right, I see now: everyone has to begin somewhere.

'He might not mind that. I mean, *then* I would have achieved something definite. The thing *is*,' – I drew a deep breath and came out with it – 'well – it's just that politics rather *bore* him.'

They were silent. Boredom with politics was a state of mind they could only comprehend intellectually. Aunt Lilian wrote pamphlets – mandated territories was her special subject – for the Fabian Society, and Aunt Kit had stood for Labour, though unsuccessfully, in the 1945 election.

'Don't you like Richard?' I asked plaintively.

'Of course we do, dear,' Aunt Lilian said at once.

She was not really against marriage, not even against mine.

Unlike Aunt Kit, who believed it to be a barbaric rite, intolerable between reasonable men and women, Aunt Lilian, the headmistress, simply felt it her duty to point out that a career – any career – would be less easy once a girl was lumbered with a husband and children. (Though in fact she would not have said 'lumbered', not because she was afraid to put forward an unpopular view, but because she was an honourable and exact woman. If she suspected she had enjoyed her life more than most of her married contemporaries, she would never have used a pejorative word about the married state, since she had no personal experience of it.) And with me, perhaps, she was even more cautious than with her sixth form girls who had mothers to put the other side of the argument. Aunt Lilian was aware – more than Aunt Kit was aware, anyway – of what might be thought a young girl's natural pre-occupations, and it was she who took me to buy clothes and lipsticks, asking the sales girls' advice with a gentle humility that touches me now, because she was not humble by nature and thought an interest in personal adornment the mark of a trivial mind. But she respected what she did not know: when Richard came to visit she always made elaborate – and sometimes embarrassing – excuses to leave us alone together.

'Richard is an absolute charmer,' Aunt Kit said. 'Of course, we both adore him.'

There was no reason why they should not. Richard has great charm, when he chooses to exert it. I had been touched by his kindness to my aunts, though later on it seemed more like arrogance than virtue. He bestowed his charm upon them like a beautiful and unexpected present: since they were old, the giving of it flattered him, not them.

'It's just that you're so young,' Aunt Lilian said gently, over the immeasurable gulf that stretched between her sixty years and mine.

'Twenty isn't young. *Honestly* . . .' I looked helplessly at their innocent, familiar faces: Aunt Kit's so ravaged and white, Aunt Lilian's so smooth, plumped out with age where

Aunt Kit's had fallen in. I loved them and longed to please them.

'At least finish your course, get your degree,' Aunt Kit cried.

But even this I could not do. I had no choice: of this they were thankfully ignorant. I could not present them, at fifty-five and sixty, with the same situation they had had to face twenty years earlier when my mother had come home from the teacher's training college where she was a lecturer in medieval history, given birth to me, and died of it.

I had met Richard when he came into the estate agent's where I was working during the university vacation. He had just been de-mobbed from the Army, intended to go up to Oxford to work for his Doctorate in the autumn, and was looking for a house for his mother who had recently been divorced. I took him to about twenty houses and had made love to him on the splintery boards of about half of them before he decided that this was not a suitable town for his mother to live in – too quiet, too far from London – and the estate agent, whose car had been left standing in leafy side-streets for too many unprofitable hours, gave me a week's wages and said he thought another job might suit me better.

I was an articulate, busy girl, brave as anything on the platform, but timid about love. Or what I thought of then as love. Until now, I had avoided sofas and the backs of cars, though sometimes I dreamed of dark rapists in romantic situations. I had always imagined that when I finally lost my virginity, it would be for the same reason I smoked and drank, because it would have seemed unsophisticated not to. In fact, the only social folly I committed was to pretend I understood about contraception. The circumstances being what they were, Richard must have known I did not, but since he knew almost nothing about me except that I was willing, he could hardly have been expected to care.

We did not know each other. It was that, I think, that excited me: making love to a stranger in deserted houses.

We found a flat in Oxford. My baby was born. Aunt Lilian sent me accounts of local political meetings cut out from the *Gazette*, and her own analyses of the Labour Government's foreign policy. Aunt Kit never wrote, it would have shamed her to write my married name on the envelope, but she knitted for the baby, strange, holey garments that stretched to a huge size when I washed them, big enough for a prize boxer. One matinee jacket arrived with a cigarette burn in the middle of the back. My aunts seemed very far away, faded, sepia photographs stuck in some childhood album. I told comic stories about them to Richard's Oxford friends – my own had drifted away and I didn't mind, seeing them through Richard's eyes as too solemn, too dull, always discussing the balance of payments – and felt no twinge of guilt. Though I still argued at parties, defending Sir Stafford Cripps and the Labour Government, no one I met now seemed to be interested: they listened to my opinions because I was pretty, their eyes on the cleavage of my dress.

Richard got his Doctorate, and decided to become a schoolmaster. He turned down a job in a famous public school and wrote to Aunt Lilian, a long, very high-flown letter, saying that he believed social segregation in education to be totally wrong and that he could have no part in perpetuating it. He had hoped to impress her, and, though I knew this was the wrong way to go about it, since she was always embarrassed by emotional arguments, when she replied in a stiff, rather guarded way, I was deeply hurt on his behalf. I decided that she had never really liked Richard and wrote her an angry letter attacking a Labour politician I knew she particularly admired, saying he did not care for Socialist principles and was no more than a cunning man who would do anything for power. Answering, she matched my silly spite with careful, sensible remarks; politics, she said, was the art of the possible and a good man, once in power, might find himself forced to do some things not quite in accord with his principles, but this did not mean he had forgotten them, nor that he would not act upon them the moment he practically could. I must try to think for myself, she went on, and *not pay too much attention to the arguments overheard in the bread queue*. This favourite phrase of hers, meaning uninformed opinion, seemed to underline her contempt for the situation in which I had placed myself: the young, married woman, abdicating intellectual effort, doing nothing but washing and cleaning and caring for her baby. I sent back a tirade of bitter invective, written during a long, lonely evening when Richard was dining in college: did she think that because I had given up working for my degree I was necessarily isolated from intelligent thought? A university education, after all, was no more than other people telling you what to think, the pouring in of examination facts, an uncreative process leading to sterility, not freedom. *I*, on the other hand, was free as I had never been before: free of the boring business of examinations to be got through and jobs to be found, I was forming my life into a growing, organic design, normal and beautiful.

The rage and hatred I felt as I wrote this letter was terrifying, like a sudden, violent illness. I shivered as if I had an actual fever, smoked a dozen cigarettes and drank half a bottle of Cyprus sherry. When I heard Richard on the stairs, I emptied the ash tray into a drawer: he never smoked himself and disliked my doing so.

Aunt Lilian said she was sorry she had upset me. She had certainly not meant to, and she was glad I was happy. Happiness, I knew, was not something she thought much of as an end: it was as if she had said, *I'm glad you don't mind being poor*, and, although when I replied to her, it was only to tell her about the baby, Thomas, and how he had put on five pounds and had cut his first tooth, I brooded over what I might have said while I stood at the sink or pushed the pram, making great, windy speeches in my mind, venting on my absent aunt the curious, unreasonable anger that seemed to rise up before me like a dark pit, bottomless and frightening.

I had no reason for anger. I had meant what I said about

19

being 'free', and though I see now that young women often use this argument as a retreat from struggle, a kind of laziness, I did not see it then. I was caught up in a closed, warm world of physical pleasure. I enjoyed Richard who was a casual, almost brutal lover, his desire rising and spending itself as impatiently as mine, so that I did not have to suffer all that tedious, preliminary business of fondling and stroking, and I enjoyed my baby, which surprised me as I had not expected to. I was very strong and he never tired me: sometimes I carried him on our afternoon walks instead of taking the pram, just for the pleasure of feeling my arms ache under his weight. The weight of least resistance – I carried him to tire myself, the way some people rush into activity when their plans fail.

If I sometimes recognized this, I blamed my Aunt Lilian who had brought me up to give too much importance to careers and causes and things of the mind, simply because she had never known, herself, any of the pleasures of the body, and had, as a result, made me feel guilty now.

On my twenty-first birthday, she sent me a cheque for three thousand pounds that had been left to my mother in her godfather's will. She said I had not been meant to have this until I was twenty-five, but since I was married and had a child, they had been able to break the trust. Now Richard was leaving Oxford, it might be hard, at first, for us to manage on his salary.

I saw this as a contemptuously charitable gesture. My aunts disapproved of inherited wealth. They had done this because I was a poor, weak creature, a parasite, incapable of standing on my own feet. I sent the cheque back, saying that although it had been immensely good of them to bring me up, I must have been a great burden and was now a disappointment, so I would prefer them to keep this money as some repayment for all they had done. I showed Richard the letter and he handed it back without comment. It was not until Aunt Kit rang me up, three days later, and abused me for ten minutes between tearing bouts of coughing, saying that I had hurt 'poor Lil' quite unbearably, that he said I had been wrong to write it.

I was astonished. 'Aunt Kit was *drunk*,' was all I could manage.

'Poor dear,' he said gravely, though he was – and still is – a terrible prude about women drinking.

I raged at him. Why hadn't he told me what he thought at the time? Oh – how I despised hindsight moralizing. This was our first quarrel.

He went white. 'But my love. . . .'

'Don't call me your love. You sound like a character out of Jane Austen.'

'Elizabeth. Don't be ridiculous. How could I have told you? It might have looked as if *I* wanted the bloody money!'

He has always cared what things 'look like' to other people.

Chapter Three

Fez, at sunset, is a golden city. Looking down from the terrace of our modern hotel, I saw the walls catch fire. Behind me, Richard said to Flora that one should, really, be staying at the Palais Jamai, in the old town.

Richard is often afraid we are staying in the wrong place, have chosen the wrong country for a holiday, are, in some way, missing something. He has an ambitious appetite for life. But he was not discontented now: we had been in Fez two days and he was airing his local knowledge to impress Flora, who had just arrived.

Flora smiled without speaking. That was one of her habits, I remembered. At Oxford, it had often discomposed me, as if I had said something foolish or affected, unworthy of comment. She had been Flora Latter then; she had become Flora Pickthorne and later on, Flora Dove. The young man with her was neither of the men who had temporarily lent her their names: too young to be a discarded husband, he was too old to be a son.

'Doctor Livingstone, I presume,' he had said when they first appeared on the terrace and Flora had darted over to us with glad, accented cries: '*Richard*, *Elizabeth*, what an *extraordinary* thing!' His remark, delivered, in a weary, satirical voice, had made me notice at once how young he was, though I would have noticed soon enough, I suppose, even if he had not made it. He was young and very beautiful; brown hair springing back from a broad forehead, blue eyes dark as pansies, a smooth, curling, sulky mouth. Beside him, Flora looked *dusty* – a paper flower left too long in a shop window.

They were lovers. They had first spied us from the balcony of 'their' room. It was unreasonable to feel shocked by this, I thought, watching them from the edge of the terrace as they sat at our table and Richard ordered drinks: a young woman with an older man is not even a cause for surprise. But that is because love is a social emotion, not a biological one: young women don't love sagging bellies and grey hair, they love money and power which men have to offer more often than women do. Flora, of course, has power of a sort. I wondered if this young man, whose name was Adam Springer, wanted to get into journalism or television, and then felt ashamed. Perhaps, after all, he was in love.

Certainly he looked sulky enough as Richard took all Flora's attention, setting out to please. Earlier, my husband had been slumped in his chair, furtively picking his nose behind a detective story: now he was sitting upright, looking bright and alert and ten years younger, telling Flora that the Palais Jamai was a really marvellous old palace, an excellent example of Moorish architecture – Richard is often a little didactic. Flora must see it. Perhaps we could go there for a

22

drink later? Although it had been converted into an hotel, it hadn't lost its atmosphere, wasn't at all *touristy*.

'You're a tourist, aren't you?' Adam Springer said. What was meant as a joke came out rough and surly: he sounded like an injured child.

'I'm glad we stayed up here,' I said. The light was fading on the walls of the Imperial city; I gave it one last look and came, reluctantly, to sit at the table. 'It's cooler and cheaper. Besides,' – I caught Richard's eye – 'the Hobbs are staying there.'

'Who are the "Hobbs"?' Flora asked, speaking their name with a comic intonation.

'Nobody. Oh – dreadful people.' Richard laughed but I could tell he was alarmed. Suppose we went for this drink and the Hobbs greeted us? Flora might think we were friends. I saw him redden: he was ashamed to have thought like this.

'They are immensely rich,' I said, to give them status. 'They have cars with chauffeurs and stay in the best hotels.'

Flora smiled. '*We* stayed in the most terrible place in Casa. A kind of *morgue*.'

'We had cockroaches in our hotel in Meknes,' Richard said, not to be outdone.

'I expect it was owned by a Frenchman,' Flora said. 'The Moroccans are terribly clean.'

I thought of the children in the casbah with flies crawling on their eyes but I was afraid to mention this in case Flora thought me naïve. I had been afraid of her at Oxford where she had been a quick, intense, thundery girl who rarely bothered to talk to other women. Now she was successful, she alarmed me even more. She reviewed for the Sunday papers and appeared on television in a programme called *Talking After Hours*, giving her views on art, morals, current affairs. I knew I had nothing to say that could possibly interest her.

Not that there was any need for me to speak. Flora was writing a book on the position of women in North African societies. She spoke about it at length and Richard asked intelligent questions. Adam Springer and I sat silent, smoking to comfort our inferiority.

There were a few other English couples in the hotel: they lay round the pool all day like slabs of meat. Now, after the daily roasting, they stayed indoors, avoiding the mosquitoes that dive-bombed in the dusk. The only other people on the terrace were a young soldier with a handsome girl in a brown djellebah. She had pulled down her veil as she sat down, hitched up her skirt to show pretty feet in high-heeled shoes, and lit a cigarette.

'It's a matter of prestige among the *bourgeoisie*,' Flora was saying. 'I daresay that girl wears a bikini on the beach, but her father will make her go veiled in Fez. Berbers are different. The women don't wear veils, though high-class Berber women are often secluded. Their men shut them up at home; even if you visit the house, the women don't appear socially. Just to serve the food.'

Her voice held the indignation that any Englishwoman would naturally bring to this subject. But she spoke to Richard, not to me. If she is concerned about the position of women, she should be concerned about *my* position, I thought. The formation of this remark in my mind encouraged me greatly and I found myself smiling. Looking up, I saw Flora's young man was watching me. He ground out his cigarette and asked, in an undertone, 'Have you known Flora long?'

'She and Richard were at Oxford together.'

He glanced at my husband with apparent distaste. Richard's back was half-turned to us. He was leaning forward, absorbed in what Flora was saying.

'When it comes down to it, it's a class thing. If you're poor, your women can't be secluded, they have to go out to work. So it's the educated women who suffer. The only ones who have any chance of rational conversation with men are tarts. Well – of course *that's* true of all masculine-dominated societies.'

Adam smiled bitterly. It made him look about seventeen. I felt my age ascending as his dropped: I was old enough to be his mother.

'We had a flat in Walton Street.' (What age can this boy have been then, for heaven's sake?) 'We used to give parties, people brought bottles of Algerian wine. We used to make great bowls of raw onions soaked in vinegar and sugar. We ate them with cheese. Flora used to come.'

He received this innocent information with a scowl. I wondered if I had offended him in some way. Perhaps by my middle-aged presence, the suggestion that Flora and I were the same age? He lifted his head and stared at me. His eyes were blue and perfect, with beautiful, white, smooth lids, like petals. I shrank from his perfection into the shadow beyond the light, grateful for the darkness. My feet ached, I had a pain in my stomach. I was falling apart. He stared as if he were meditating an assault on me.

'Did you know we were going to meet?'

'*What?*'

A second later, I saw that this question had no psychic implication. It was simply that he had begun to fear we had arranged this with Flora: as if, in his mind, he could hear her saying, *oh yes, what a splendid idea, I shall be bored with young Adam by Fez. . . .*

'Of course not,' I said pityingly. 'Why, we haven't seen Flora for years.'

'When was it?'

'No idea. London?'

His voice was muffled. He stood naked by the open balcony door, towelling his head after a shower. Below us, the city twinkled; jewels in black velvet. A dog barked and barked.

'She was married to Pickthorne. They had a flat with a garden.'

I remembered, very dimly. A narrow, dusty yard, smelling of cats. Warm gin and tonic in heavy glasses. Our Tom, and

Flora's little girl on a red rug. Heads wobbling on pale necks, like heavy flowers. Toddling? Crawling?

'Was Oliver born?'

'You were pregnant.'

I was surprised that he should sound so definite: it was usually I who pinned down occasions with that sort of fact. I was pregnant; that was the year Tom had measles, Nonni had her operation.

'It *was* Pickthorne then, not Dove?'

'Positive.'

'Who was Dove, anyway? What happened to *him*?'

'She left him. He was an awful man.' He hesitated. 'He assaulted her daughter when he was drunk.'

'How frightful.'

'Yes.'

I was puzzled. 'I'm sure we didn't see her again though. Not after we left London.'

'Maybe not.'

'Then how . . . ?'

'Oh, I heard somewhere or other. I can't remember.'

He dropped the towel. His face was red from the day's sun and his ears were scarlet.

'She certainly looks her age, doesn't she?'

'Why on earth shouldn't she?' He watched me, smiling but sharp, and for some reason – for no reason – I was reminded of a time at school when I had tried to make one friend betray another, and failed.

'She's a bit rough on that poor young man. She treats him like a lackey.'

'Jealous?'

'Of course not.'

'Angry, then. Don't be angry.'

He came up and touched my breast through my night-dress. He grinned at me and tweaked the nipple. I moved away and said it was too hot. He turned his back, took his pyjamas off the bed and put them on.

'I have a pain,' I said to his turned back.

26

'I'm very sorry.'

'Perhaps it's the water. I daresay you were right, I shouldn't have brushed my teeth out of the tap.'

'You had your period at Gibraltar, a headache in Tangier.' Richard spoke in a detached, schoolmaster's tone: it sounded to my ears, unkindly mocking.

'Yes,' I agreed, used to this situation and, for the moment, accepting the blame for it. Tears burned hot in my eyes. 'I really do have a pain.' It was true now. 'Excuse me,' I said, aggrieved, 'I have to go to the bathroom.'

When I came back, he was in bed, reading. 'You should have taken those pills.'

'I know.' I lay in the bed beside him and stared at the ceiling. It was very hot. The dog was still barking outside. I stretched out and touched his arm. 'It's nice here, isn't it?'

'Lovely.'

He turned a page and cracked the spine of the book.

'If you do that, the pages will fall out. And I haven't read it.'

He closed the book at once and put it on the bedside table. 'Oh, don't be *silly*.'

He picked the book up again, not looking at me. I sighed heavily and he took no notice. I thought: why should he? It wasn't his fault. Nor mine either, come to that. How can you be blamed for something that isn't your conscious fault? For *not* feeling something? There is this terrible guilt, though. Sometimes friends have talked to me, confidential over lunch-time gin. I listen but I don't talk about myself – I like to think because I believe in privacy, but really it's because I'm too proud to admit failure. And too embarassed. *Is* it my fault? For most of the time his prancing and moaning leaves me inert and contemptuous. To pretend would be despicable – or would it? It's easy for a woman.

'You can if you want,' I said ungraciously.

'Not specially. Thanks all the same.'

There was a time when I used to try to make it work by lying still beside him beforehand, and thinking of someone else. No one I knew well, just one man or another, seen in the street or at a party. Is sex, for me, something I only want with strangers in the dark? Not with someone close, someone I love?

'I do love you,' I said, like a child touching wood.

He turned his head and smiled at me. 'I love you, too.'

I smiled back gratefully, and went to sleep.

I dreamed of Richard. He had left the fire on in the spare room. I went in and found the room stifling. Wasting electricity. *Wasting electricity*, I shouted, my mouth stretched open, stiff with rage. Then Richard was sitting on the sofa in our drawing-room. It was winter; there was a fire spurting blue gas in the grate. Tom was lying on the hearth rug, reading *Flipper*. There was a woman on the sofa beside Richard: as I watched, he pushed her down beside him and lay on top of her. I couldn't see her face but I knew she was older than I was. Her skirt was rucked up, showing an expanse of mottled thigh above her stocking top. I said, 'The joint is burning,' and Richard turned to smile at me, his hand on her breast. Tom sat up and looked at them. Then he looked at me.

I woke up. Richard cleared his throat dryly and turned a page of his novel. I lay still, hot with anger. Richard had never done anything like this, nor would he: even if he had been unfaithful to me – though as far as I knew, he never had – he would never humiliate me publicly. For some reason, this realization disappointed me. I closed my eyes, pretending it had really happened. I saw myself leaving the room, packing a suitcase, writing a note. *Elizabeth behaved with great dignity. She wrote: I thought it would be less embarrassing for the children if I were not here.* The pathos of it all was thick in my throat. *Elizabeth made no fuss, screamed no reproaches.*

'What's the matter?' Richard said.

'I had a dream.'

'Bad?'

I swallowed. 'I dreamed I wished you were dead.'

'As long as it was a *bad* dream.'

'Oh – don't laugh.'

'I wasn't. I just thought it sounded healthily normal.'

'Normal?'

'Well, I should imagine most husbands – most wives – wish each other dead, sometime or other. Subconsciously, of course.'

'Oh,' I said. 'Oh. Yes, of course.'

Chapter Four

'That's where it shows,' Flora said, slapping at the loose skin of her under-arm. '*There*, and under the eyes.'

She peered appraisingly at herself in the mirror, pulling faces as if she were alone, and I was embarrassed by her candour. (Though I have as much interest in my appearance as most women, I feel it is somehow degrading to admit it. Before we came away, I bought a special cream supposed to restore elasticity to the skin, but I destroyed the wrapper on the jar and the accompanying, incriminating literature, as furtively as I had, when young, removed the cover of a book on sex.)

Perhaps, I thought, sitting on the bed and watching Flora, perhaps I feel like this because I am ashamed to be a woman, a member of that subjugated race whose preoccupations are so trivial and unimportant.

Flora has no such inhibitions. Successful in a masculine world, she has the confidence to be feminine when she feels like it.

'I suppose', she said, with one last, earnest look in the mirror, 'it's something to be almost done with the bloody

decades. Perhaps one should have an artificial menopause
and be done with them altogether. A new life at forty! I
believe it works marvellously, as long as you keep up the
hormones.'

'You don't look forty.'

At this moment she didn't. Flat-chested, narrow-hipped,
her fair hair sleek from swimming, she looked like an impish
boy.

She looked at me. The slight attack of dysentery had tired
me and I had slept most of yesterday and again this morning.
Now, after lunch, she had come up to fetch me.

'You look marvellous in white, you should wear it all the
time,' she said, and smiled at me. She has a charming smile,
very generous and merry: since there were no men present,
I got the full benefit of it. 'But why don't you wear your hair
down? It would make you look so much younger.'

'I like to be tidy.'

She looked round her. 'Perhaps that's why your room
seems so much nicer than our's. Young men make such a
mess, they're so *lordly*.'

Totally deflated now, I smiled at her brightly.

'Sure you feel well enough to come?' I nodded, and she
put her hand on my arm as we left the room. 'Richard says
you're doing such marvellous work with your old people. I
want to hear all about it.'

I felt she was condescending to me – like a don condescending to some poor don's wife at the annual garden party,
asking about her social work, her charitable committees.
But I was grateful for her interest, so I explained about our
Council's scheme: the converted houses where the old ladies
and gentlemen live, each with their separate apartments,
their own furniture, but a common dining-room. 'One housekeeper can look after about ten old people, as long as they
don't get really ill. That's the problem – each house has to
be economically independent after the preliminary conversion, you see, so we can't afford nursing staff. We try to get
continuity of care by links with the local hospital – we're

very lucky at the moment because we have a good geriatric doctor who visits with the almoner and tries to put off taking them into hospital as long as possible. When they *have* to go in, he's there, it means it's all less terrifying, less alien, and they have a better chance. And of course we keep their rooms for them as long as there's any chance at all – it's tremendously important that they should feel they've a home to go back to.'

(But three houses – which is all we have so far – can only take in thirty old people. There is Mrs Abercrombie, ninety years old, on the waiting-list for seven years and making her daughter's life hideous. *She makes my tea with the same water she boils the eggs, she says she don't but I know better and you know what that does. Egg water brings warts, you drink it you get warts on the stomach. Amy, Amy –* this in a stentorian roar, because Mrs Abercrombie is very deaf – *Amy, I've told the lady on you, she says she'll have the police round if you don't watch out. . . .* Mrs Abercrombie has been incontinent for the last year and is unsuitable, now, for one of our houses. There is no room for her in the geriatric ward either, or won't be, until Amy dies, which may not be long. The last time I saw her she looked yellow and thin – as if she were made of some dry, friable material and would crumple into sand if you touched her.

There are hundreds of Mrs Abercrombies, hundreds of Amys. What good are three houses? It is like trying to ladle out the sea with a sieve.)

'It sounds terribly interesting,' Flora said. 'I'd like to hear more sometime. Your's isn't the only scheme of this kind, is it?'

'We aren't supported by any national organization, if that's what you mean. The idea started in our Care Committee – we raise half the money for the conversions, the Council supplies the other half.'

Flora looked thoughtful. 'Richard thought it might be a good idea if I wrote an article for *The Guardian*.'

Bless Richard. *Damn* Richard. Flora's article would do

more good than months of jumble sales, bring-and-buy fairs, charity fêtes. I stamped on ugly resentment and said, humbly, that I would be very grateful. I could give her all the facts and figures.

'Just the relevant ones, duckie.' She smiled kindly, but her eyes had already gone beyond me, to Richard and Adam waiting under the eucalyptus trees, by the swimming pool. As we approached, her smile flashed like a lighthouse beam. 'Have we been *ages*? I'm so sorry.'

'The car's come,' Richard said, to me. 'Better?'

I nodded, though just walking downstairs had made my head spin.

The hired car we had ordered stood outside the hotel. We got in to drive down to the medina. Flora sat in the front with Richard, Adam beside me, at the back.

'*Sure* you're all right?' Adam asked. His blue eyes rested on me with, apparently, genuine concern. Swimming seemed to have washed away his sulkiness; he was smoothed out, ready to charm. A young man with a pleasant, feral smell, whose bare arm brushed against mine. '*I* had a nasty turn last night. God – I felt as if my guts were falling out.' For the rest of the short journey, he discussed his symptoms with the self-absorbed vehemence of a young man to whom pain is a single, shocking insult, not feared as a forerunner of something worse. I told him he could have some of the pills Richard had got me from the chemist yesterday. They seemed to work, but left one rather wobbly.

'Do you still feel wretched, Adam darling?' Flora turned and laid her hand on his knee. She was always touching him, as she touched everyone. She called Richard and me *dear*, *darling*, *duckie*, laying her small, cool paw on our arms.

(I find it hard to show affection in this way, even with my own husband, my own sons. They say young monkeys brought up apart from their parents have no confidence in sexual matters because they have never observed the adults making love. Except at the cinema, I never saw a man and woman kiss each other, until I was grown up.)

32

We passed little shops hollowed out of the walls, selling henna, mint, aromatic seeds. Richard and Flora walked ahead with the guide, a tall, elderly Arab with a contemptuous, burnished face, wearing a brown robe. I trailed behind them, looking at a fountain, a mule piled high with skeins of brilliant, dyed wool, at children monotonously working shuttles in a weaver's shop. Adam craned his neck to look after the others.

'You go with them,' I said. 'It's just that I can't understand French. Anyway, I'd rather *look*.'

Still prepared to be charming, he agreed. 'All that information – stuffing it in like geese. What will they do with it, after all?'

'Flora is writing a book.' But that wasn't really the reason. Some people like to know, others prefer to look. The lazy ones, like me.

'As long as we don't miss the mosque,' Adam said, and took my hand to hurry me on, like a character out of *Alice*. We saw the others ahead, waiting in a tiny square with a fountain and a single tree.

Richard said impatiently, 'Don't you want to see the university?'

I shook my head. I felt giddy and sorry for myself. I am usually so well that I bear even mild illness badly. 'I'll stay with you,' Adam said.

I was glad he had spoken as if he wanted to, but I felt I should apologize, once they had gone. Bad enough that Richard should have annexed his girl friend, without being left with Richard's boring wife. . . .

'They've got a lot to talk about, they used to know so many of the same people,' I said, to comfort him.

He looked surprised. 'God, *I* don't mind. As long as you don't.'

We walked slowly through narrow, sloping streets, covered from the sky by some kind of matting. I was happy to be with this handsome young man. One shop had rolls of hideously patterned linoleum outside. It was very crowded;

33

two men came down the street, straddled on a trotting mule, and people pressed against us. We passed the mosque and saw, through the gateway, men washing their feet. Not being Muslims, we were excluded. 'Look,' Adam said, 'for Christ's sake, Elizabeth, will you *look* at those ceilings.'

He looked down at me. It was all disconnected, like a dream. 'In here,' he said, sometime later. 'Here' was a small palace, a courtyard and a fountain. Low seats, darkness and coolness. We sat down and he took my hand. Someone brought mint tea in a silver pot, on a chased, silver tray. Adam traced the design with his finger. 'It's never perfect,' he said. 'There has to be a fault in the pattern somewhere. It says so in the Koran. It's presumptuous, you see, for it to be perfect.'

'Did Flora tell you that?'

'I told *Flora*.' He laughed softly, with pleasure, as if I had fed him the right cue. 'Flora doesn't know anything. She's just a mass of opinions – when you dig down, it's *amazing* how little she knows. Frightening, really, when you think of her on the goggle-box, laying down the law.'

'Don't be jealous.'

'Oh – I'm over that.' He spread out my fingers on his knee. 'You've got pretty hands.'

My hands are ugly. Large and boney, they show my age. I removed my hand gently, and used it to lift my glass of tea.

'What do you do?' I asked, like a mother.

'Work at the B.B.C. That's just for bread, of course. I'm writing a novel.'

'What about?'

'People.'

'If you were writing about animals, it would be a fable.'

He grinned at me. 'I like you when you're tart. Your eyes shine. But it was a daft thing to ask, wasn't it? I mean, what *are* books about?'

'In our library, they're classified under Crime, Romance and General.'

'*God*. I suppose writers have to get used to it.'

He looked gloomy, weighed down by the burden of his chosen profession. He took my hand again. 'I don't know what you'd call mine. It's about a young man who's in love with an older woman. She's got a husband and five children. I think he kills her in the end, the young man, I mean.'

'Oh.'

He looked self-conscious. 'It's not autobiographical, if that's what you're thinking.'

'I'm glad. If he does murder her . . .'

He laughed as if I had said something annihilatingly funny and kneaded my hand gently against his thigh.

I felt ashamed because I was enjoying this sensation. I leaned back weakly against his warm shoulder and closed my eyes. 'Elizabeth,' he said, and then, a moment or so later, with a different intonation, 'Elizabeth. I think there's someone here who knows you.'

Mrs Hobbs was wearing a tent of stiff, pink linen. Her husband looked uncertain. I introduced Adam. 'A young friend of ours,' I said, trying to sound as if it was the most natural thing in the world that we should be sitting here, holding hands. Mr Hobbs gazed at me as if fascinated. His wife sat down and, after a brief hesitation, he followed her example. More mint tea was brought.

'Funny stuff, isn't it?' Mrs Hobbs said. 'Rather refreshing though, when you get used to it. What's been happening to you? We thought we might see you yesterday.'

I explained about the dysentery, and she urged me to put my feet up.

'Get all the rest you can, in this heat.'

'You must drink bottled water only, and not touch the salads,' Mr Hobbs said.

'Hark at him! He doesn't take his own advice, I can tell you. Nothing but lettuce, lettuce, lettuce, just like a rabbit!'

'My stomach's hardened,' Mr Hobbs said. 'I have travelled a lot in the East.'

'Where have you been, sir?' Adam asked politely. (A good-mannered boy, just out of school.)

'Only Japan. About ten years ago.'

'The Japanese are a very clean people,' Mrs Hobbs said, it seemed obscurely. 'And the girls must look so pretty, though Mr Hobbs says they wear modern dress now, most of the time. Did you see *The Tea House of the August Moon*?'

I shook my head. Mr Hobbs said, with pride, 'Mrs Hobbs has a professional interest in the theatre. She used to be in the front line at the Windmill.'

'*We never closed*,' Adam said. 'Isn't that right? All through the war, the Windmill kept open. My mother told me.'

'I was an old married woman by then,' Mrs Hobbs said. 'Only not as weighty as I am now, of course.'

'Mint tea is not really the best thing for you,' her husband said. 'There must be about half a pound of sugar in that pot.' He gave a little cough and looked at me. 'I fear Mrs Hobbs pays only lip service to the cause of weight reduction.'

'I've got a dreadfully sweet tooth.' She giggled suddenly: sweat stood on her forehead like seed pearls. 'Still, you know what they say, Daddy? Sweets to the sweet. . . .'

'Sweets to the sweet, farewell,' Mr Hobbs said. 'I thought thy bride bed to have deck'd, sweet maid, not to have strewn thy grave. It comes from *Hamlet*.'

Laughter tightened inside me like a pain.

'Mr Hobbs is a great reader,' Mrs Hobbs told me.

'I expect Mrs Jourdelay is familiar with the quotation,' Mr Hobbs said. He stood up. He wore a silk shirt with a cravat tucked in round his thin neck, and elegantly uncrumpled linen trousers. He said, to Adam, 'Mrs Hobbs fancies a souvenir. I want to look at that stuff they've got over there. Like to come?'

They went to look at the jewellery piled on a table on the far side of the courtyard.

'It's fairly pricey in this sort of place, I expect,' Mrs Hobbs said. 'But we're off tomorrow. How long are you staying?'

'I'm not sure. Two days, three perhaps. . . .'

'Daddy can't wait to get over the Atlas. For myself, I'm

36

not fussy, though the dogs do bark at night, don't they? Tossing and turning, I couldn't get a wink.'

She looked very tired. There was a faint blue-ness about her mouth. When she stopped talking and smiling her face sagged, the flesh falling away from her chin and dropping into the white folds of her neck. She leaned back, her head resting against a red and blue carpet hanging on the wall. Her eyelids drooped.

The men came back across the courtyard. Mr Hobbs put two bracelets down on the table, heavily carved things, very pretty. 'Which one do you like the look of, dear?'

She woke up with a little start, wiping the corner of her mouth with her hand. The debate was prolonged and earnest. When it was over, he slipped the chosen bracelet on to her dimpled wrist, smiling into her eyes like a lover.

He looked at me and seemed to hesitate a minute. 'May we give you the other one?'

'Oh *no*.' Taken by surprise, I protested clumsily. 'You can't – you hardly – I mean, they're terribly *expensive*.'

'You can't take it with you,' Mrs Hobbs said.

I found myself blushing. I put the bracelet on and waved my arm to show them. They smiled at me, as if I were a favourite daughter.

'Go on, say thank you nicely,' Adam said.

The dream-like feeling continued. We left the palace and parted from the Hobbs. Mrs Hobbs had to rest before dinner.

'I have to be careful of her,' Mr Hobbs said. He stood, thin and elegant beside her, a willow supporting a mountain. 'I hope we meet again.' I thought he looked at me sadly.

'Parting is such sweet sorrow,' Mrs Hobbs said. 'It's been lovely meeting you, hasn't it, Daddy?'

A lump came into my throat: this was a sentimental occasion. I took her little hand and kissed her soft cheek. She smelt – curiously – of toffee apples. Some kind of childhood smell.

'I'm glad you did that,' Adam said, when they had gone. He looked ridiculous, solemnly approving me. *Me!* Old enough to be his mother! 'They're sweet,' he said, 'but Flora would have laughed at them.'

Oh, he wasn't so young, I thought. At least he had grown beyond the need to despise people in order to give himself stature.

'It was nice of him to give you that bracelet. It cost a simply huge amount. Still, I daresay he can afford it.'

'You don't know that.' I felt indignant at this casual assumption. 'They may have saved up for this holiday for years.'

'You know KWIKCLENE, the dry cleaners. Well, he *owns* them. At least, I think so. I asked him what he'd been doing out East and he said he'd been starting up a chain of these shops in Japan.'

'I would have said he was a Bank Manager. Or a minor civil servant. Though it's impossible to tell, really. What does a Funeral Director look like on holiday?'

Adam laughed and tucked his hand under my arm. We strolled through the little streets. My giddiness had gone and I felt happy and relaxed, as if I was being carried along on a slow, peaceful current. Adam held me just above my elbow, stroking the inside of my arm with his thumb. 'Shall I stay,' he asked suddenly, 'or shall I go?'

It seemed a strange question: I wondered if I had mis-heard. I didn't reply because all at once we were caught up in a crush of people who seemed to erupt from nowhere, running, pushing against each other. We were in a narrow street with high, blank walls and the sun beating down. A mule clattered past, its straw panniers thrust us against the adobe wall. Behind the mule came more people, running and shouting. Adam held me steady against the wall, protecting me with his body, very pleasantly. In the circumstances, it was reasonable he should hold me like this.

A man yelled something. Adam frowned. 'I think there's a fire. Don't be frightened.'

38

'Those matting roofs in the market! They'll go up like paper. . . .'

I affected more fear than I felt.

'It must be several streets away. We're all right here,' he said, holding me closer still. It became apparent that he was as aware of me as I was of him. He gave me a self-conscious grin and then yelped as someone thumped him in the back. 'We can't stay here. I think there's a doorway back there.'

He half carried me. The doorway led into a small court with white walls and flat roof of red earth, empty except for a man sitting on the ground on a blue mat. He was an old man with blue eyes and a hawk's nose, wrapped in a white robe like a bundle of washing. Adam spoke to him in French. The old man answered, shrugging his shoulders.

'He says it often happens, they'll put it out soon,' Adam said.

He was still holding my arm but there was space between us. Too much space and too much light in this courtyard: it made me think of the difference between his face and mine. I wished I had something to offer him – charm or eccentricity. 'What do we do now?' I asked, laughing vivaciously.

'That's up to you.' He spoke meaningfully. His eyes had a blue, brooding look.

'Well—we can stay here till the panic's over, or we can go out and be trampled to death,' I said, pretending to misunderstand him. I looked at the old man calmly sitting on his mat and hated him, knowing – knowing myself – that nothing would come of this. If only we could be transported instantly to some Eastern couch, in some dream, out of time. . . .

'I've finished with Flora,' he said. 'I'd made up my mind to go.'

I laughed again. 'Has Richard put your nose out of joint? It doesn't mean anything, Richard only likes to talk.'

'It's nothing to do with your *husband*,' he said, with charming pomposity. 'I knew it was a mistake before we got to Fez. She's bored with my juvenile conversation.'

I saw the sense of this, though regretfully: there is very

39

little real communication that can take place between one generation and another. But it was foolish of Flora to have told him so.

'I was going home, but I'll stay if you want me to.' He watched me intently, eyes narrowed against the sun which struck into this side of the courtyard, waiting for me to give a reasonable answer, which was foolish of *him*. I should have liked to go on as we were, but nothing goes on, even for a short time, without making the kind of decision which was, in this case, clearly impossible. What could I say, asked outright? A woman of my age, with principles, used to making practical arrangements, qualifying statements, weighing things up?

'As I said, it's up to you,' said this stupid young man, who could have done anything he liked to me – or so I felt at that moment – if only he had *done* it, and not talked about it first, trying to strike a bargain. I hate to say something I don't mean, and I had enough sense left to know I might not be prepared to keep my side of the contract tomorrow. Not that it would have mattered so much: we could have gone on, wrangling over terms and leaving the outcome to chance, and there is, after all, quite a lot to be said for anticipation. But I knew he might not take this view – it is only hindsight that makes you take it, and he was not old enough for hindsight.

I said, with my ridiculous laugh, 'Dear Adam, I can't see it *is*. We won't be here much longer.'

'We could share the car, it would be cheaper,' he said, but he was looking doubtful now. Wondering if I had, after all, missed the point?

'The car's small, it wouldn't take four people. Not with luggage as well.'

I felt this was a sad moment, a sad valediction, and yet, behind the sadness, was a kind of relief. Did I really want this young man – oh, not now, this minute, pressed on top of me – but tomorrow, and the days after, breathing down my neck?

'I suppose not.'

He looked resigned but not too gloomy. I thought: I shall regret this lost opportunity longer than he will.

'When will you go then?' I asked.

'Tomorrow. I'll tell Flora when we get back and I'll catch the train in the morning.'

He did his best to look reproachful, but he was already cheerful underneath.

He kissed me in the back of the car while we waited for the others, but nothing moved in me. Apart from a super-ficial, tactile pleasantness, I felt nothing at all.

Chapter Five

Adam did not appear at dinner. Flora wore gold ear-rings shaped like Grecian urns, and dark glasses. To hide red eyes? She sat in gloomy silence, pushing her food round her plate.

'Why the wake?' Richard asked, when the dragging evening was over.

I told him. 'I suppose she didn't feel like talking about it. It's her own fault, really. She's been foul to poor Adam.'

'Poor Adam?' He looked quizzical, one eyebrow arched.

Of course he was right. It is seldom the old who seduce the young. Though I argued with eloquent indignation – *Flora had only brought Adam along to carry her luggage, book rooms* – I knew this in my heart.

My mother was thirty-seven. She was quiet and serious but very passionate underneath, Aunt Kit says, rather like

Emily Brontë. Aunt Kit is intensely romantic. My mother's picture shows only a drab, mouse-like girl with timid eyes. She got a first at Girton and taught, for most of her life, in a girls' boarding school. She never met any men until she met the young man whom I cannot think of as my father. He was a student at the teacher's training college where my mother, in her thirty-sixth year, took a job as a lecturer. She thought he had promise and offered to coach him, in the evenings, for a university scholarship.

'Of course he would have married her, he was very devoted,' Aunt Kit said, deceiving herself, I think, since he made no attempt to see my mother after she had resigned from the college and come home to her sisters. Whether he would have done the right thing by her – as they said in those days – is fruitless speculation: he was never told of the need.

'We thrashed it out and decided it would be quite wrong to burden him, on the threshold of his career.' Aunt Kit told me this rather aggressively, so I think the implacably moral – and romantic – decision was almost certainly hers: she has the nature for high-minded renunciations, grand gestures, and had, at this time, already taken to drink.

I have no evidence of what my mother felt. 'She was always very quiet and withdrawn,' was all Aunt Lilian would say, when pressed, and perhaps her interest really was in the young man's academic future, not in her own, or mine, because she continued to coach him by post until two days before my birth. And her death.

He got his scholarship. When Aunt Lilian wrote to tell him of my mother's death – she said she had died from pneumonia – he sent a wreath of lilies and a letter, saying that if it had not been for her tuition, he would not be where he was now.

Nor would she have been, if it had not been for him.

Flora, of course, was nothing like my poor little mother, nor was her situation comparable, but one cannot help being affected by memories, however irrelevant they may be, and, thinking of that other middle-aged woman deserted by her young lover, made me sorrier for Flora than I might otherwise have been. I would have been sorrier still if she had not paraded her distress so openly, sighing and staring into space and insisting that Richard should buy her whisky, which is expensive in Morocco – in her place I should have been so humiliated and ashamed that I would have done my best to put a good face on it – but I was sorry enough to agree that she should come with us, in our car. In fact, I suggested it before Richard did, though it was obviously in his mind first – had been, almost certainly, from the moment Adam left. The day before we were due to leave, he came up to our room after lunch and began by saying that perhaps it wasn't so sensible for Flora to continue her journey by herself, travelling by local buses across the Atlas, and not only not sensible but not altogether *safe*, even though she was tough and independent and used to looking after herself. I knew what he was getting at, of course, and I was so hurt that he should think he had to approach me in such a roundabout fashion – as if I was a terrible, uncharitable woman who had to be coaxed into a simple act of kindness – that I suggested it myself at once, though it was really the last thing I wanted.

I suppose, too, that I felt guilty: if I had behaved like a properly loving wife and refused to let Flora monopolize Richard so blatantly – which I only did because I was enjoying Adam's company – the situation might not have arisen.

Chapter Six

There are great chunks of life, after childhood, which drop out of conscious memory. Until we drove up and over the Atlas, I had not thought for years about our time in London. But to travel is to set the mind free. I sat in the back of the car while Richard drove and Flora talked; the car established rhythms; the landscape flowed past; I looked out of the window and felt my thoughts flow too, relaxed and liberated.

Apart from that one lunch party, I could not remember meeting Flora at all. We must have done because they talked, as we drove, of common friends we had had at that time, but I remembered none of them – or only a name, here and there.

My memories were different.

We had a first-floor flat. I had to drag Tom's pram up eighteen steep stairs. Our bedroom curtains were made of brown hessian. Apparently, the flat had been previously inhabited by giants: I am tall for a woman, but all the shelves were too high for me to reach without standing on a stool. There was a bathroom with a sloping floor and an ineradicably evil smell: even in winter, with the snow drifting in, we bathed with the window open.

The cost of this hideous place was enormous. We could have found somewhere cheaper, or taken up Richard's mother's offer that she should buy a house in the suburbs and share it with us, but Richard had theories about the importance of a good, central address, as well as about the waste of nervous energy involved in travelling. To help pay the rent, we let a back room to a nervous queer with pale, bulging eyes, who was a friend of a friend. He burned joss sticks in his room, a practice Richard objected to, though it improved the smell of the flat.

I was alone all day except for the baby. I made friends with a girl in a similar plight: Sophie had twin boys the same age as Tom, and her husband, Jack, ex-R.A.F. with a handlebar moustache, was working for his exams in chartered accountancy. Sophie was a pint-sized ash blonde with tiny hands and feet: carrying her plump, placid babies, she looked like a wren with two cuckoos. She had been an actress in a northern repertory company and missed the life: she was as bored as I was. We became 'best friends' as schoolgirls do, pushing our babies to the park together on fine afternoons and on wet ones, sitting in each other's flats drinking whisky – how we afforded it I cannot now imagine – while our babies played behind the sofa. Babies and boredom, boredom and babies: when the whisky ran out, we made up our faces, exchanged clothes, did our hair, and the afternoon still yawned ahead. We had all this unused *energy*, that is the main thing I remember. Some evenings, we left our husbands to mind the children and went to the Palais or to the skating-rink, tearing round and round like young colts let out in the meadow.

We were bored with our husbands. They were sober young men, marking school books, studying, advancing into an adult world of action and responsibility. We were silly girls, forced by our situation to be idle, thrust back – or so it seemed to me – into childhood games of playing house. We met men: 'spivs' as they were called then, at the corner café; medical students at the skating-rink; a rich Australian who slept with two women at once and who suggested, one evening, that we should come and watch; a Greek, old at thirty with a sad, soft face, who took us to his family house in Belgravia where we played gramophone records in a pale, cold room with a high ceiling. We had, not love affairs, but intrigues; giggling over trysts at the skating-rink, kisses in taxis.

Richard disapproved of Sophie. He said she 'used' me. I thought he was simply jealous of the time I spent with her, instead of sitting on the other side of the gas fire, knitting or darning socks while he marked his school books.

Sophie had a young doctor whom she used to call in to her babies. He came one afternoon when one of them had a cold. It wasn't bad enough, really, for medical attention, but Sophie was bored. While he bent over the cot, she watched him with a mischievous look; after a little, she said she had a curious pain in her chest. He hesitated a minute and then asked if she would like him to examine her. With an abstracted look, she removed her sweater and brassiere. She was one of those deceptively fragile girls who look plumper naked than clothed: she had beautiful breasts. The doctor sounded her chest, asking questions about the pain, and all the time trying to keep a sober, professional look though his hands were trembling and in the end he had to sit down to conceal his excitement. He said there was nothing wrong with her chest, but the baby should have a prescription. The shops were closed this afternoon, but if she would come to the surgery now, he could make it up for her. Would I – they looked at me vaguely – mind staying with the children?

That afternoon, various incidents that had puzzled me at the time, became clear to me. I didn't blame Sophie, understanding her position only too well, but if sex was her way out, it wasn't mine.

I began, slowly, to disentangle our relationship. I was in the early stages of pregnancy, so skating was no longer a sensible pastime. We still had coffee together in the mornings, pushed our babies to the park, giggled together. We discussed Sophie's affairs: I discovered, in the process, some interesting sexual practices I had not known of before which she did not indulge in with her lovers, in order, as she put it, 'to keep something for Jack'. She was a girl of firmly fixed, if limited, principles, and, on the purely domestic front, an excellent wife. She cooked superbly, adored her baby sons and mothered her husband, buying him linctus whenever he

46

coughed and insisting he should take cod-liver oil in the winter. I don't think Sophie had ever felt anything so complicated as guilt, so she must have done these things because she was fond of him. 'I'm fond of old Jack, I wouldn't want him to be hurt,' she would say with a sigh when we discussed the difficulties of meeting her current lover without Jack finding out. She was such a sweet-natured, generous girl – I had never before nor have I since met anyone so naturally, if indiscriminately, kind and loving – that I found it hard to deny her anything. Though we no longer went out together in the evenings, I promised to keep up the pretence that we did.

Since I had to do something during the hours I was supposed to be with Sophie, I joined the local Labour Party. That I didn't tell Richard, was partly for Sophie's sake – to say she had become interested in politics would have been stretching his credulity too far – but also for my own. Richard seemed to me to have changed so much, become humourless and uncertain-tempered, a family man who grumbled because his socks were not mended and his shirts not ironed properly, so that I was slightly nervous of him and also resentful: I felt that I had become, in his eyes, so much a *wife*, that he would see my new involvement as a nice occupation for me, like embroidery or dressmaking. Of course, in thinking like this, I was doing him a great injustice: the change was not so much in him, as in the way I saw him.

And, though I hate to admit it, the fact that I saw him differently was Sophie's doing. Men, to her mind, were puppets to be manipulated; if you were 'clever', they would do what you wanted. This attitude is not uncommon but it was new to me, as were a good many of Sophie's ideas, and because of its novelty I think I was unconsciously moulded by it: I had begun to see Richard as someone to be 'got round', a duped enemy rather than a husband.

I fell into deceit quite easily, having got used to it over the past months. I told myself it was only for a while. At the

47

back of my mind, perhaps, was a kind of childish vanity: there is a lot of dull, humdrum work to be done in local politics and I felt Richard would not be impressed if he knew I was abandoning him three nights a week in order to address envelopes or collect jumble. I wanted to be sure I could establish myself, become 'somebody', before I told him what I was doing.

That is always a mistake, of course. Once you begin lying, it is hard not to go on because it is impossible to explain why you lied in the first place. A friend once told me that she had never told her husband she was Jewish. She hadn't told him in the beginning because it was totally unimportant to her – her family was not religious – and then, after they had been married a while and she had discovered he was extremely intolerant about various classes of people – not Jews, in fact, but Negroes and Catholics – she had been afraid to tell him in case he should think she had deliberately concealed her origins because she had not trusted him.

Of course, at first I did do all the humdrum work, though to be honest, I never found it dull. The shabby room above the tobacconist's shop where we held our ward meetings became home to me and, in a queer way, made me feel whole and integrated again so that I began to look back on the activities I had taken part in with Sophie as some kind of mental aberration. Though perhaps it wasn't so queer. There was such a deep gulf between the stern, dutiful world of my aunt's upbringing and my schooldays, and the kind of lotus-land I seemed to have fallen into during the last year, that I had sometimes felt, when I bathed my baby or sat giggling in the park with Sophie, that I was taking part, not in real life, but in some wildly unrelated dream.

There was a general election pending at this time and it seemed certain we should lose it. There was a lot of criticism of the way our party had conducted the present government; this, combined with the fact that our constituency was a safe Conservative seat, meant that we had a shortage of enthusiastic workers. Not that the atmosphere was gloomy: it is a

48

curious fact that as a general election approaches, excitement builds up even in the most hopeless fight. You know a miracle will not happen but you find yourself behaving as if it might: we canvassed, those weeks before the election, with a heady feeling that success was round the corner.

It turned out that our candidate, who came to address us one evening, knew my Aunt Kit and had the greatest admiration for her, even though he also knew that the only reason why she had not been offered another, safer constituency after 1945 was that it had become too obvious she was unable to keep off the drink. We talked about her for a long time, and I think our Chairman was impressed. At any rate, at the next ward meeting, he suggested that I might like to stand for the local council.

We went to the pub afterwards, to discuss it. Like our poor parliamentary candidate, I would have no chance of being elected, but it would be a beginning, though perhaps one I would have despised several years earlier when I looked down on parish-pump politics and intended to be the first woman prime minister. There were, on the other hand, a lot of interesting points at issue, the most important being the use the present council was making of the housing subsidy. I have forgotten the ins and outs of it: all I remember is that we argued as passionately as if the national survival was at stake. Our Chairman was a master printer, older than I was but an extremely good-looking man, so that my excitement had a sexual side as well as a political one. As a result, I drank more than was sensible in my condition: like a lot of women, I always felt more unwell during the first three months of pregnancy than afterwards, and alcohol went to my head very quickly. When the pub closed, the Chairman insisted on walking me home.

Richard was waiting on the steps of our converted house, a dim shape by the open door. He remained there, out of the man's sight, while he said good-bye to me. When I came up to him, he stood stiffly aside so I could precede him up the stairs. Once inside the flat, the storm broke.

49

'Who is he?' he kept repeating over and over again, stony-faced and disbelieving even when I had told him the truth. As luck would have it, Sophie had had no arrangement of her own for this evening, and, either forgetting our pact, or not taking my need for it seriously as she knew my activities were, on her terms, so innocent, had dropped in to borrow some coffee. Naturally Richard had asked her where I was and when, realizing what she had done, she said I was at her flat, he had telephoned Jack and discovered this was untrue.

At first, of course, Richard did not believe me. Understandably, perhaps: women who deceive their husbands in order to attend political meetings are probably rare, even when they hold, as Richard and I did, different opinions from each other. When he did see that I was speaking the truth, he was bewildered and hurt. This made me feel a quite genuine shame and remorse although – it was as if I was torn into two separate parts both rationally and emotionally – I knew that hurt bewilderment was something I should beware of: he was my enemy who would use any art to outwit me if I could. He said that I must be mad not to have told him. 'For God's sake, what am I? A kind of monster? Don't you know that all I want is for you to be happy?' This was true, in a way, and his saying it made me sympathetic and tearful, but on the other hand I knew that if I *had* told him, his attitude would not have been as indulgent as he was pretending now. There were endless ways in which he could have made my activities seem a nuisance, positively damaging to our marriage, or – which would have been worst of all – merely trivial.

He went on for a long time – we had such *energy*, then, in our quarrels – and sank deeper and deeper into what was really absurdity, saying that it was all his fault, he had been a lousy husband, too absorbed in his job to notice I was bored and fretting because I was 'wasting my education', and that if only I had been 'straight' with him, we could have done something to put this right. Then he began to change his ground, to slip from real remorse into disguised anger, saying that he should never have trapped me into domesticity, meaning, of course, that I should never have trapped *him*, and, instead of getting angry underneath – as I had earlier when he was being honest with me – I felt an enormous, trembling sympathy with him and begged him to stop: he wasn't, after all, responsible for *everything*. *I* had been stupid not to trust him, *I* had behaved badly, disregarded and neglected him. I was a bad wife, I couldn't even cook or look after his clothes. I broke into violent tears at this point, I remember, and flew upstairs to turn out his drawers, looking for socks with holes in them. He followed me, almost in tears himself, and said that he didn't give a damn for his bloody socks. He would go barefoot, rather than see me unhappy.

This made us both laugh. We collapsed, laughing, on to the bed; we were young enough, still, to forget our differences in that way. Richard did not really forget though. He came home from school some days later and said he had been 'thinking very seriously about our situation' – he was already beginning to be pompous – and that it was quite obvious that some women were unsuited to a life which held nothing but home and children.

He produced this with solemn pride as if it was a new and revolutionary idea: it was, in fact, an unfashionable one. This was the immediately post-war period when, presumably because of the years they had spent in the services and munitions factories, there was a great movement for women to return to purely domestic functions. All current thinking supported it. Articles appeared in the press extolling the creativity of 'home-making'; psychiatrists warned that children who grew up without their mother's constant care and attention were seriously deprived and might well become delinquents.

'Of course,' Richard said, 'you could only work part-time because of Tom and the baby. That's the important thing. Household chores will present a bit of a problem, of course, but the children matter most. I daresay if we get someone sensible to look after them a few hours a day, they won't suffer *too* much. What we really need is someone who *loves* them, who'll be constantly *there*. Of course that's impossible in the flat. I wonder, now, whether we were really sensible to turn down Nonni's suggestion. . . .' He hesitated a minute. 'I know you were against it, and right to be probably, but it does seem the only practical way out of the difficulty – she does adore Tom, you know, and she's dreadfully lonely. . . .'

He had been against it, too. Apart from the bore of travelling in from the suburbs every day, his mother irritated him. It crossed my mind that if he had changed his opinions it might be partly because the squalor and expense of the flat – made worse by my bad housekeeping – had begun to get him down. (It had surprised me to find how fussy he was about some things; dust, and scrappy meals really bothered him.) But since he seemed to be thinking only of me, I felt this was an ungenerous idea.

I said nothing; he took my silence for agreement.

'It would be nice to have a garden, wouldn't it?' he said enthusiastically. 'Healthier for Tom, and fun for us too. We could grow our own vegetables. *Asparagus* . . . ! What I'd like would be a biggish house, Victorian, perhaps. The proportions are good and we could make a separate flat for Nonni. Victorian houses are a bit of a drag on the market just now – too big for most people – so we should be able to get one quite cheaply, particularly if it's a bit run-down. With a bit of conversion and a lick of paint, some of these old houses can be splendid to live in, lots of room to breathe, not like a modern box. It would be fun if we could find some mock-Gothic ruin and do it up, wouldn't it?'

He seemed to be bouncing ahead of me, in great, lighthearted jumps, like a ping-pong ball. If, deep down, I felt a warning rumble of panic, I disregarded it. After all, he was thinking of my future, abandoning all his theories about convenient flats in London, near to his job, for *my* advantage.

'Once we get everything organized,' he said, 'you can become a career woman.' He beamed on me like an indulgent father promising a marvellous present off the Christmas tree.

Chapter Seven

We stopped in a dull village on a plateau. People stood on street corners; thin dogs sniffed at refuse; there were graphic warnings up, outside the post office, about syphilis and T.B. There was only one hotel, owned by a Frenchwoman, and even this was only nominally open. This Government, she told us, was determined to drive out foreigners. She let us have two rooms but there was no visible staff, and the dining-room was closed: we ate, that evening, in a shabby bar in the middle of the town. A notice on the wall said that it was forbidden to serve drinks to Muslims and a television set flickered in the corner. An Arab Perry Mason interrogated a woman in a yashmak while Flora told us, indignantly, that the blood money for homicide among some Berber tribes depended on the sex of the person killed. 'Murdering a man will cost you forty sheep, murdering a woman, only twenty!'

'Disgraceful,' Richard said, and winked at me privately. I ignored him. How could he assume I should find Flora's feminist outrage amusing? *Me* – reared on John Stuart Mill and Mary Wollstonecraft! Flora might sound ridiculous, but she was right. Richard's wink, his comfortable, masculine amusement proved it. No doubt he would like to be a Muslim with four wives all dedicated to his comfort. Wasn't he enjoying this journey, with two women competing for his attention? If we had been alone, he would have complained bitterly about the hotel. Instead, as we walked down to the bar this evening, he had been all smiles and indulgent gallantry, complimenting us on our appearance, an arm lightly circling each of our waists. 'Girls', he called us, 'girls', enjoying his situation: it was as near as he was likely to get to being a pasha in a harem. An old man, I thought, flattered and dreaming.

Flora seemed ruffled. Her ear-rings shook in an agitated way as she finished her wine; then, eyes downcast, she traced a stain on the table cloth. Had she seen Richard wink at me? A married couple can stand back to back like warriors facing a circle of enemies; it is hard if you are only one. Like any smug, married woman, I was sorry for Flora.

'This veiling of women,' I said, 'is it to keep them chaste? Do they make much fuss about that?'

'Only in the Rif and the northern part of Algeria.' Brightening, she held out her glass to Richard and he poured her more wine. 'The Berbers in central Morocco are much laxer – closer to some traditions of Mediterranean antiquity. They're a randy lot, really – they only murder unfaithful wives if they actually catch them at it.' She looked at me, slightly surprised, as if she had not expected me to be interested. 'Mostly, so far as I can tell, they turn a blind eye. In some Berber tribes, pregnancies are believed to last any period – a good deal longer than nine months, certainly. I suppose this was originally to give a sterile wife a period of grace – she could tell her husband she was pregnant but owing to the machinations of some female rival, the child was "asleep".' She grinned, and for once took one of my cigarettes. 'Naturally this belief has other uses, too. I believe that when the French were here, a man could enlist with the forces and still claim paternity for children born during his absence, even if he'd been away a couple of years.'

'It seems a useful concept.'

We both laughed. Flora is pretty when she laughs, I thought, and was glad there was this sudden sympathy between us. I had really been rather lumpish and dull during the drive from Fez: perhaps Flora had thought I hadn't wanted her with us? To show this was not true, I began to talk to her in an animated way, and she was attentive, encouraging me with questions. I knew Flora cared no more about my opinions than about the opinions of the rather derelict Arabs, drinking Coca-Cola at the bar – probably a good deal less, in fact, since theirs would be useful copy for her – but she was kind enough to pretend that she did, drew me out and flattered me until I felt witty and successful and told outrageous stories about people we knew. Richard, who had heard them before, frowned and swatted flies: it grew very hot. The Frenchwoman who ran the hotel came in with a crowd of people and sat at the only other table. 'Let's go back, it's suffocating here,' Richard said.

We walked out into the dark street. Richard went ahead, hands in pockets. Flora and I idled behind. The evening had seemed to float by. I had tears in my eyes from laughter.

Flora said, 'It was a pity you didn't take that job.'

'What job?'

'*You* remember.' She laughed; we were like old friends. 'Of course it was ages ago. Years. It just came into my head, I don't know why.'

'You're thinking of someone else.' It seemed a queer conversation.

'No. Richard . . . !' He turned, waiting until we caught up with him. 'Richard – tell this wife of yours.'

'What about?' He stalked warily beside us, like a hunter.

'That job.' She staggered a little and put her hand on his arm. 'Oh God, I think I'm drunk. Did we have a lot to drink?'

'Only one bottle between us,' Richard said.

'It was years ago. At a party. You said Elizabeth wanted something to do. She needs an outside interest, you said.'

'What party?' I asked, but neither of them seemed to hear me.

'I went to a lot of *trouble*,' Flora said, aggrieved. 'Rang up all sorts of people. Then when I found this job and told you about it, you said she really couldn't manage it. She had too much to do with the new house and the new baby, you said.'

'What job was it?' They were looking at each other. I felt cut off, a fish mouthing behind glass.

But Flora had heard me. 'On a weekly. I knew the editor. He wanted a secretary – not an ordinary girl, one who knew about politics, current affairs. It would have suited you down to the ground.'

Why didn't she name the paper, I thought. Did she think I didn't read?

Richard said, 'I didn't tell you. It really was impossible. I thought you'd only fret over it.'

'When was this, anyway?' I felt embarrassed: clearly we had seen more of Flora at this time than I remembered. I said, apologetically, 'It's ridiculous, but I only remember our meeting once, after Oxford. Our babies were tiny. Do you remember?'

'Of *course*.' Flora sounded warm and eager. 'It was the most marvellous, hot day. James thought you were the most delicious creature he had ever seen.'

'James?'

'Pickthorne,' Richard said. The word dragged out of him as if speech was an effort. I had a sudden feeling of unplaced alarm, a shadowy fear in the darkness.

'Oh, we met lots of times after that,' Flora said. 'At parties and things. I daresay you didn't notice me.' She smiled, her hand warm on my arm. 'I was never the centre of attention, like you.'

'I'd begun to hate parties when we lived in London. All those people shouting at each other. I could never think of anything to shout.'

I thought, pleased: I am old enough to admit this now.

'You always looked happy. Didn't she, Richard? Absolutely *surrounded* by the most attractive men.'

I saw myself: a great, blowsy open flower, men buzzing round like bees.

56

'It sounds all right. I don't remember it.'

'Oh *duckie*.' She laughed, it was a challenging sound like a peal of bells. 'I can remember being madly jealous.'

'I can't believe that,' Richard said. His voice was rather thick, not very amused. He walked between us, linking arms.

Neither could I believe it. I couldn't think of any situation in which Flora could be jealous of me. All I could see of her was the tip of her nose on Richard's other side, bobbing backwards and forwards as she walked, like a bird eating grain. The image came into my head; she wasn't like a bird, more like a squirrel, quivering-nosed, bright-eyed, chattering on. . . .

'You're not very gallant to your wife, Richard,' she said.

'I could hardly be, to both of you.' He was looking down at her. He squeezed my hand.

'She was lovely though, wasn't she? Beautiful as the day.' Her voice had a dying fall.

'Talking of past glories,' I said. 'Did you know Mrs Hobbs was once at the Windmill?'

'What? Oh, my *God*.' Richard's disbelieving laughter echoed in the thin air.

'Truly.'

'I can't believe it.'

His wonder seemed stupidly exaggerated. 'I expect she was very pretty when she was young.'

He heard the annoyance in my voice and answered, mockingly, 'Why are you so sentimental about them?'

'Am I?'

'Yes, you are.'

His arm had stiffened against mine. We were both rigid as enemies, longing to come to blows. I didn't want to quarrel in front of Flora – it seemed humiliating over something so small – so I said, 'Well, it's just that they seemed so happy and fond of each other. Enjoying themselves, like children at a fair.'

Richard groaned.

'Why didn't I meet them?' Flora asked in a social voice.

Chapter Eight

There is only one road over the mountains and down to the desert, so it was stupid to assume – as I had done, without really thinking about it – that we should not see them again.

But I could not have foreseen the circumstances. Though when we came on their car, somewhere on the long, dirt road to Tinerhir, there was no time for surprise. Only for the sickening leap in the throat, the feeling of being frozen in the moment of falling.

Richard was out of the car before I could open my door. The heat struck like a fist. I ran after him, stumbling in the red dust.

Mrs Hobbs was lying at an angle to the car, her head under the chassis, her body stretched across the road. She looked like a white rock; a pillar from Stonehenge, fallen. Her legs were covered with a white shirt; beneath it, her feet stuck out, pink, puffy, in biege sandals. I stared at her. This was all meaningless, like a film when you come into the cinema halfway through.

Mr Hobbs said, 'It was the only thing I could think of. The only shade. The car's like an oven inside.'

He had rigged up a sort of tent, I saw now, draping his jacket over the open door, a shirt over her legs.

'Have you broken down?' I asked. 'I could only think of stupid, unimportant questions. 'What happened to the car?'

'The car can wait,' Richard said. 'She's passed out. It's probably heat exhaustion.'

'Salt tablets,' I said, and Mr Hobbs stared at me. He was pale, his long, hollow face looked blank and idiotic.

'In the boot, in the small green bag,' Richard said. 'Don't run in this heat,' he added sharply, as I started back to our car.

Flora helped me open the boot. We found the salt tablets and a bottle of mineral water. Everything was covered in fine, red dust that gritted between the teeth. 'Will she be all right, do you think?' Flora asked. 'Dear God – what a place to choose.'

There was no shade anywhere. I had thought of the desert as sand, but it was stone; red stone and harsh dust and a wide, stone sky. Descending from the mountains, we had seen patches of pale, rasping grass; pink oleanders in dry stream beds; black, low, nomads' tents. Here there was nothing but emptiness and stone.

Mrs Hobbs was half conscious. She mumbled something while Flora supported her and I wiped her face with the warm, fizzy water. I tried to crush up a salt tablet in a cup and dissolve it in the water but she moaned when I held the cup to her lips and tried to turn her head away.

'She's too heavy, I can't hold her,' Flora gasped, and Mr Hobbs took her place, supporting the heavy, lolling head on his bony shoulder. Flora had moved her, rucking up her skirt. He pulled it down, stroking the material smooth, and took her hand. 'It's all right, dearest,' he whispered. 'You'll be all right soon.'

He looked at me despairingly. 'It's too hot – I should never have brought her.'

The sweat was running down from his hair line and trickling into his eyes. He had no free hand. I leaned across his wife and wiped his forehead with my handkerchief.

He smiled pitifully. 'I'll never forgive myself.'

'She'll be all right,' I said. 'Once we get to the town, there's bound to be air-conditioning in the hotel. What went wrong with the car?'

'Dirt in the carburettor,' Richard said. 'It won't take long, but she'd better not stay here. You and Flora will have to go on, take her with you.'

Flora was driving our car towards us, bumping over the ruts. A cloud of rose-coloured dust flew up behind it.

'We'll have to lift her,' Richard said.

Flora held the door of the car open. Mr Hobbs dragged at his wife, his breath whimpering.

'I think we can manage it,' Richard said. 'Elizabeth . . .'

We bent, hoisting her arms, like limp, white tree trunks, over our shoulders. When Nonni had her strokes, we had learned how to lift her, taking the weight on our thighs. This woman was twice Nonni's weight. We linked wrists beneath her knees; she lolled on our stretched arms like a great bundle of washing with a body in it, the victim of some obscene murder. 'Easy now,' Richard said. We inched towards our car, muttering instructions at each other like a pair of furniture removers used to working together. We perched her vast behind on the back seat and rested, gasping. I tried to push her knees round but there wasn't enough room; I was wedged in the doorway, her arm still half round my neck. My muscles hurt; I couldn't endure any more. My breath came in little whines, like a dog dreaming.

Mr Hobbs appeared in the opposite doorway, hauling at her shoulders. He had a bald, egg-shaped top to his head; it was surrounded by a little fringe of grey hair, soft as a duck's tail. He pulled her backwards on the seat. She was white as her dress.

'You'd better get moving,' Richard said. 'As soon as she comes round, get her to swallow those salt tablets. Does she have any pills for her heart?'

'She took them when we broke down. She can take them again in' – he consulted the gold watch on his wrist – 'about an hour's time.'

He looked at me helplessly. They were all looking at me: Richard frowning; Flora blind in dark glasses.

'Take him with you,' Flora said to me, 'I'll stay with Richard.'

Richard nodded. 'Can you manage? It's the best thing, really.'

I got into the driver's seat and started the car. 'Good luck,' Richard said, at the window.

Mrs Hobbs lay on the back seat. Her husband edged in,

lifting her head on to his lap. I drove off, jolting past the stranded car.

Mr Hobbs said, 'I don't know how to thank you.'

'I'm only glad we came along.'

'I didn't know what was wrong. I've never had anything to do with cars.'

'Neither has Richard, professionally,' I said curtly. It seemed ridiculous that anyone could not clean a carburettor. Then I saw his face in the driving mirror and felt ashamed, as if I had struck a child.

'We don't have a car of our own,' he said humbly. 'At home, we go out so little.'

'What happened to the chauffeur?'

'He disappeared at Erfoud. I should guess he just wanted to get there. It wasn't the hire company's fault,' he added meticulously. 'I took him on myself. It was purely a private arrangement.'

The sun struck through the open window on to my bare arm. 'You'll get burned,' he said. He hung his white shirt, the one that had covered his wife's legs, over my arm.

'Mrs Hobbs talked a lot about you,' he said. 'She's always wanted a daughter. Not that she doesn't adore the boys and of course they worship their mother. They didn't like the idea of her taking this trip. I should have listened to them. I don't know what I was thinking about.'

It seemed pointless to let him go on reproaching himself. 'What was it like at Erfoud?' I asked, to divert him. 'It's the real desert there, isn't it?'

I couldn't remember why we had decided not to go there.

'Beautiful,' he said slowly and rather shyly as if this was an emotional judgment he was ashamed of admitting to.

'What you expected?'

'Far beyond.'

Our eyes met in the mirror.

'Space,' I said. 'Thousands of miles stretching away. Like being on the edge of the world.'

'More like another world altogether. Of course, I'd read

about it. Flecker and Shelley. "Lone and level sands" – that's Ozymandias, you know – but it really gives you no idea. No idea at all.' He seemed surprised as if it had not occurred to him that literature might let him down in this way. 'We could see what looked like a range of hills from our window but they'd gone by the morning – nothing left but huge ripples as if a great tide had come up and washed them away. It made me feel – oh, I don't know.' He hesitated. 'As if nothing that I'd ever done mattered, only that I was here, part of the earth, at one with it, as they say. It was a most curious experience – spiritual, really,' he said, speaking formally and rather quaintly. Then he coughed a little as if he had embarrassed himself and went on, returning to his normal, slightly facetious manner, 'Though not one Mrs Hobbs cared for, I'm afraid. She found the flies troublesome.'

His wife stirred on his knees. He bent over her whispering, 'Better now, my love? My poor girl . . .'

She made a dry, moaning sound.

'Try giving her some of the water,' I said.

There was a *pop* as he released the spring clip. 'Could you possibly go a little slower?'

I eased my foot on the accelerator, watching for each hole in the road that stretched ahead endlessly, a straight, straight line across a desolate land to the reddish horizon.

'She's taken a little. It's all right, my darling, Mrs Jourdelay's driving us. No, don't talk, just rest now. Daddy's here, looking after you.' He added, in a lower voice, 'How far, do you think?'

'I don't know.' I tried to visualize the map. 'Forty miles?'

He sighed.

'Maybe not quite so far,' I said.

We advanced slowly, on this desert of stone. Peering ahead, I could sense the whole world turning. I thought about Adam and held a conversation with him in which everything turned out differently. I thought of Flora and Richard. He was saying to her, *Of course, they'll be all right with Elizabeth. She's marvellously competent, you can always trust her in an emergency. I know she seems indolent on the surface, but underneath she has all this energy, like a coiled spring. It's devastating, really. She has this hidden strength. . . .*

Maybe this wasn't Richard, but someone else talking.

I thought of Flora and her two ruined marriages. Pickthorne was thick-lipped; a heavy, solemn man like a bulldog. He was something professional – a solicitor, an accountant? Had he really called me a 'delicious creature'? It seemed unlikely. *Elizabeth has always had a low opinion of her physical charms.* Pickthorne had played, most of the time we were talking, with his baby girl whose name I couldn't remember. Why hadn't I asked Flora? She had talked to me about Tom and Oliver, but only, it seemed, because she thought my children were all I was likely to be interested in. Like some grand lady, condescending. Perhaps she would, really, have liked to talk about her daughter. Had the next husband really assaulted her? How old would she be now? Older than Tom – about eighteen. What shall we do with Tom, if he doesn't get into a university?

Of course, Flora is attractive, but Elizabeth has more real charm. And I should guess, though maybe there's no real evidence of this, a better mind, clearer, more incisive. . . .

Richard graded people on an examination system. 'So-and-so has a second-class mind,' he would say when we were first married, dismissing one of my friends or another. His friends all had 'first-class minds'. He made me feel as if he had rescued me from some intellectual gutter, some abyss of boredom. I had not thought my friends dull, but he had made them seem so. Why had I listened to him?

The trouble with Elizabeth is that she is over-modest. She cannot believe that what she thinks about this and that has any value, because she has thought it. It is a kind of deep humility, really. . . .

The sky had clouded over; the cloud coming up from the desert and spreading over the whole wide sky in a matter of minutes. A cold, harsh light struck through deep wells in the banks of cloud; then these wells filled up and it became almost dark. The rain came suddenly and a hot wind, as if someone had opened a furnace door, hurled it against the car. We wound up the windows as quickly as possible but we were already soaked. A gritty fog surrounded the car; the sand rattled against the windows like small hail. Some of it got into the car and irritated my eyes: I had to take a hand off the steering wheel to rub them and it was almost wrenched out of my grasp as the car lurched into a hole in the road.

'Can you see?' Mr Hobbs asked anxiously.

'It's no worse than driving in mist,' I said, to comfort him, though in fact it was hard to see the road; I was afraid that at any moment the car would go bumping off it, into the surrounding desert. Several times the steering wheel took on a wild life of its own as we crashed into an unnoticed pot-hole, and the windscreen wipers stuttered against the rain of dust and small stones that hurtled against the car in handfuls: it was if we were under fire.

'I hope your husband is all right,' Mr Hobbs said. 'Would you like me to drive?'

'I think we're here!'

Buildings seemed to rise out of the desert. We passed a long, low, adobe wall. It was still raining, great drops spurted up whirlpools of dust, but the buildings cut off the sand and made it seem lighter. I slowed down and children ran beside the car, a flock of skinny white birds, hopping and shouting. We passed a small public garden with tiny, stunted trees; through an arch, the road wound upwards to the hotel, perched like a toy on medieval ramparts. The car was surrounded by a circle of robed figures: we seemed to be in the middle of some whirling ballet.

Someone opened the car door. I stumbled out and the ground seemed to tilt. I went up the steps and into the hotel. It felt cold in here, though other travellers, sitting at the tables, wore only thin clothes. I wanted to find someone to help Mrs Hobbs but as I went to the desk, she was already being carried through the door. Her eyes were open now; they looked frightened and her mouth hung open. I wondered, in a cold, detached way, if she was going to die.

They got her upstairs and into a room with a large, iron bed and a lot of heavy furniture. The windows were shuttered and the electric light was on. I went to rinse out a towel in the hand basin.

She lay on the bed like a white, stranded whale. She muttered something as I wiped her face. I thought she said, 'Sand under my plate', but it seemed an unlikely remark, so I smiled, soothing her like a baby. 'Just a minute, we'll have you comfy in no time at all.'

'I think she wants to take her dentures out,' Mr Hobbs said apologetically. I eased off her sandals while he turned her head on the pillow and cupped his hand round her mouth.

It was as if he had removed her skeleton. Her face was a soft mass of blubbery flesh. We gave her salt tablets and two of her own pills; her head wobbled loosely as she swallowed. A man had brought in the suitcases and stood them in the middle of the floor. Mr Hobbs unpacked a nightdress and together we helped her out of her clothes. She closed her eyes as we did this as if she could not bear the spectacle of herself, a helpless, groaning hulk, being rolled about the bed. Mr Hobbs gave her back her teeth and she shot me a desperate little smile. 'Awful, seeing me like this,' she murmured.

'Nonsense.' I took her hand. Mr Hobbs smoothed her hair back and adjusted the pillows.

'What a horrid nuisance I am!' She was articulating more clearly now, and the colour had begun to creep back into her face.

'Don't be silly, my darling.' He touched her cheek gently, like a bridegroom. 'You gave us a fright, that's all. Mrs Jourdelay has been wonderful.'

'Elizabeth,' I said.

They smiled at me. 'I'm so sorry, a stupid, helpless old fool,' Mrs Hobbs whispered, and I felt as if there was a weight on my chest, choking me. Why should she apologize for being old and ill? (Even Mrs Abercrombie, once when

65

Amy was out and I changed her sheets, cried like a baby from shame.)

I said, 'Shouldn't you have a doctor? I can go and ask someone.'

'He'd be a foreigner, wouldn't he? Oh no, I'm all right. It was just one of my silly turns.' She did seem better now; her cheeks were pink, though patchily, and her eyes looked clear. 'I'm all right now, in this nice room. Though it's a dreadful country, isn't it, all those poor people and this terrible heat? And mile after mile of nothing, it makes you feel queer just to think of it. Like the end of the world.'

Mr Hobbs said, 'Don't talk, my love. You must rest. You know you always talk too much when you've got over a bad turn.'

'Well, it's nice not to find yourself dead,' she said, but she closed her eyes submissively as he drew the sheets up over her. He sat on the bed and took her hand. 'Rest now, my darling,' he said.

I felt envious of them. I wished Richard could see them together.

Chapter Nine

We lay in bed with the window open. Outside, a backdrop of stars glittered. It was all we could see. The room was totally dark.

'Why didn't you tell me about that job.'

'Have you been brooding over *that*. Oh, for God's sake.'

'As a matter of fact, I've only just thought of it.'

'Oh. Sorry.' He sat up, thumped his pillow, and lay down again. 'You couldn't have managed it. I can't remember exactly when it was, but I know Oliver was tiny and you'd been ill.'

'You could have told me, though.'

'What for?' He sighed; he was a voice and a querulous sigh in the darkness. 'You couldn't have taken it on, even you would have had to see that, but it would have worried you sick. You had this awful guilt about not doing anything. It made *me* feel guilty – I daresay that's why I asked Flora.' He stopped, yawning. 'Satisfied?'

'Mmm.'

He reached out for my hand. 'This is a bloody awful lumpy bed.'

Hands linked, we lay still. Outside, sprockets whirred as someone rode past on a bicycle.

'God, I'm so tired,' he said.

He and Flora had arrived three hours after we did, just as the hotel manager was suggesting we should send out a truck to meet them. The carburettor had clogged up a second time in the storm and they had had to wait until it was over. Flora had gone straight to bed and though Richard had stayed up for supper, he had been too worn out to eat much. Until now, he had barely spoken, except to tell me how tired he was.

Lying on his back, his legs spread wide, and occupying more than his fair share of the bed, he began to snore.

When I woke, the sky was clear. The air was hot and dry; it had dried my mouth. I got up to get some water and went to the window. There was a balcony outside; I climbed over the low sill and walked to the edge of it.

The terraces of the casbah fell away down the hill, dovetailed into one another like the streets and courts of a medieval city, all enclosed in a wall of the same red earth. At one end there was a little tower where cranes were nesting. Beyond the wall was the palm-grove, a chess-board of different coloured grasses, and beyond the oasis, the flat, ochre colour of the desert. The air quivered, not just far away in a heat haze, but close by me on the parapet, in a kind of vibrating brightness that hurt my eyes.

It was very still, very quiet. When I heard the clatter of horse's hooves, it seemed an enormous, ringing sound, filling the empty sky. It came from the far side of the hotel; I walked along the balcony to the far end.

The hotel was perched aloft like the bridge of a ship. From this side, I could see the modern town the French had built, outside the casbah. Red walls of baked earth, crenellated like a child's fort; neat, red courtyards; a red street with a line of palm trees down the centre. A black horse was galloping down it, frisking his back legs like a colt. A man appeared at the end of the street, shouting and fluttering his white arms: his robe billowed like a sheet on a washing line. The horse turned into a courtyard where he slowed down, trotting round the small square. More men appeared in the street and began to converge on the courtyard. Their voices rose, pure and distinct in the clear air as they laughed and shouted to each other. The horse stood as if posing for a Munning's portrait; black against red; head arched. He was small and elegant: tapering legs with a white band on his left knee. The men came into the courtyard and he began to prance, just out of their reach. They formed a circle round him and he broke out of it into a gallop, tearing round and round the square in a high-spirited frenzy. Three men stood in the entrance of the courtyard, waving sticks. Once, he galloped straight towards them but came to a stop a few yards away, rearing on his hind legs before continuing his wild circling. I half-wished he could get away – though where would he go if he did? – and was sorry when they caught him, though he seemed docile enough and stood calmly by his captor, who patted his neck as he threw his head up and down. It was as if he hadn't really wanted freedom, only to assert his right to be free if he chose, which is quite a different thing and has something both sad and comical about it.

Chapter Ten

In the way of people who have a lot to do but nothing they really want to do, I developed various minor ailments after Oliver was born. I suppose it was this that made Richard think I could not manage Flora's job.

Practically, perhaps, he was right. The house we bought, with Nonni's money, was, if not the Victorian ruin Richard had wanted, at least an Edwardian shell. It had only six bedrooms, but there was enough room in the kitchens and pantries to billet an army, though they would certainly have mutinied at the conditions there. Apart from beetles and damp there was a curious, sweet, noxious smell which took months to track down to seeping drains, and then more months to put right. The garden was full of ground elder and purple loosestrife and though Richard dug an asparagus bed, he considered weeding was a woman's job. Oliver was a whiny child, partly, I think, because Nonni had set ideas about bringing up babies which involved feeding them at set hours and leaving them to cry in between. As a result, he was underfed and cried more.

Perhaps I could have ignored Nonni's theories, but I was very unsure of myself except in matters of political opinion, and she was the sort of woman who is strong because she has never questioned her fixed beliefs: a kind of older, more battered Sophie. She had been divorced by her two husbands, deserted by her last lover, and considered herself very virtuous because she neither drank nor smoked. 'It gets into the curtains,' she would cry, rushing into rooms and flinging windows wide.

I meant to be fond of her but I found her tiring. She liked

to plan everything – meals, shopping expeditions – in pains-taking detail; she was – again like Sophie – an extremely efficient housekeeper, always turning mattresses and telling me I ought to starch table napkins and put fresh flowers in the hall every day. She had brought a lot of her own furni-ture with her and would sigh and shake her head every time she found a burn or a ring mark on it, and tell me how she had always polished her things 'until you could see your face in them'.

'We have mirrors for that,' I said once, but only once: her bewildered collapse was so shocking. She burst into tears and said she had not meant to criticize me; it was just that we didn't love her, nobody did, and she had only her 'things' to care for now.

She didn't mean – I think – that Richard and I were not kind to her, only that she did not 'come first' with either of us, and she was a woman who needed to be made much of and fussed over. Perhaps one of the reasons she had gone from one man to another was that she could not bear to lose the excitement and flattery of the early stages of love.

At this time she was just over fifty, a well-built woman with a high-coloured, sculptured face, short black hair and fine legs.

My aunts were bewildered by her. Listening to her talk about the make of corset she wore and the neckline shape that best suited her, speaking on these matters with the kind of solemnity they would only have brought to bear on the country's economic situation or the future of the United Nations, they regarded her with the polite incomprehension with which they would have looked at a Martian. Aunt Lilian and Aunt Kit walked into the nearest shop whenever their clothes became too shabby and bought the first thing that fitted them; if they debated, it would only be about a garment's staying power. Housewifely talk suited them no better. Why should anyone discuss floor polish? They had never put it on their floors. And when, to show what a good little wife I had become – Nonni thought that my aunts did not 'appreciate' me, meaning that they did not go in for endearments or tell me how pretty I looked – she pointed out, one Sunday lunchtime, how well I had starched the table napkins, Aunt Lilian said, 'But why? It seems a lot of trouble.' Nonni should have answered, of course, that they stayed cleaner longer, which would have made some kind of sense to my aunts. Instead, sensing a criticism – which this was not, Aunt Lilian was simply asking for information – she gave one of her loud laughs and said, well, she *personally* thought it was a good thing for a young married woman to cultivate the little niceties of life.

Nonni was the daughter of a prosperous dealer in scrap metal who had also been a lay preacher. She had married an insurance agent – Richard's father – and later a solicitor in a country town who had left a wife and two children for her. But the money with which we paid for the house – and with which she bought her nylons and expensive corsets – came from scrap metal: though her father never spoke to her again after she left her first husband, she was his only child and he died intestate.

When I first met Richard, he told me his grandfather had been 'a parson'. I was shocked when he told me the truth. I was disgusted by the whole idea of class and thought I could abolish it by pretending it didn't exist. I told Richard it was not only wrong but immensely stupid to lie about this sort of thing. But it was I who was stupid, too stupid to see he had reason for wanting to establish what he thought of as respectable origins. He should not have been ashamed of his grandfather, of course, but his upbringing had been pitiful, constantly on the march from one to another of a whole series of 'uncles' – there were several between his father and the solicitor – so that he had nothing stable in his life at all. He told me, some time after we were married, that when he was at school he used to show round a photograph one of his mother's lovers had taken of part of Versailles, and say it was his grandfather's rectory in Ireland.

I persuaded him to be ashamed of snobbishness – or perhaps I only taught him to keep his true feelings from me. But he remained – though I'm sure he honestly fought against it – a little ashamed of his mother. I think he felt it most when my aunts came to visit us. He would watch their puzzled, attentive faces while Nonni talked about clothes and the latest film she had seen, 'jollying them up a bit', as she called it: she thought that because their lives had been man-less, they were therefore dull and sad. My aunts, of course, thought *her* life had been tragic, and, because they were sorry for her, curbed their natural tartness and tried to talk about what interested her. This meant that for long periods they were uncomfortably silent because they could think of nothing to say. Richard thought their reserve condescending. He would redden suddenly, for no apparent reason, and chew the skin at the side of his thumb-nail.

That his distress was so foolish, made it all the more poignant. I could not bear to see him suffer and so I threw myself wholeheartedly on to Nonni's side, arguing passionately that my aunts' lack of interest in day-to-day matters was a boring affectation; that Nonni was much more 'real' and 'closer to life'.

And, since I could not admit that I often found Nonni both difficult and boring, I had a hard time with myself. It was at this period that I began to think about myself in the third person: *Elizabeth is compassionate and considerate, she thinks how other people might feel.* Though this may sound childish – and I was in fact childish in many ways, as young women are who have never had to shift for themselves but have always had someone to stand between them and the world – it did, in fact, help me to behave better to Nonni, who was not stupid at all in matters of feeling, and easy to hurt.

She was fond of me – no virtue on my part, she was an affectionate woman by nature – and wanted me to be happy. When I began to talk about getting a job she said, first, 'Do you really want one, dear? Richard and I thought you had settled so nicely' – as if I was some sort of jelly – and then, 'Well, if you really want to, I suppose it would be nice for you to earn a little pin money.'

Her kind indulgence made me shrink a little. I had grander plans for my future than that. But, though Nonni was willing to look after the babies for part of the day, even the dullest of part-time jobs was not easy to find. Perhaps it was stupid of me, but I had expected so much, if in rather a vague way, that the reality was a bitter shock: I was unqualified, I had no degree, I wasn't even trained as a secretary. It soon became clear that nothing which came up to my expectations was open to me. When I realized this, the walls seemed to close in.

I became a gloomily devoted mother. We had a big garden, but I insisted that the children must have variety in their surroundings. I never took them far from home, although I told Nonni I intended to in order to prevent her accompanying me, inventing expeditions to the common where she might tear her stockings on the brambles, or to the recreation ground which was a mile away, too far for her to walk in high-heeled shoes.

At the bottom of our garden there was a small river and a caravan site on the patch of waste ground beside it. The site belonged to a timber merchant who had consistently refused to put in adequate sanitation and drainage, finding it cheaper to pay the fines imposed instead. People said the place was a disgrace to the neighbourhood, full of immigrant Italians, thieves and vagabonds. When a mail robber was run to earth there – he was living with his sister by whom he had three little boys – the local paper was bombarded with letters from the outraged citizens of our suburban town complaining on both counts: the threat to property and the affront to public morals.

I never saw the mail robber, though Tom played with his children – and caught nits from them, to Nonni's horror – and I got to know his sister, Elsie: a thin woman with stiff, blonde hair who was never without a cigarette stuck to the corner of her mouth. She went about with her head at a slight angle and her eyes permanently narrowed, to avoid the smoke. Elsie was amiable but not very bright, and now her brother was in prison, she was in a bad way financially. 'I don't know where my next penny is coming from, I really don't,' she would breathe in her flat, light voice, as she sat hunched on the river bank, too hapless for despair, while our children played together among the drifting garbage at the water's edge.

She was behind with the rent, the timber merchant had given her notice, but she had done nothing about it – what could she do? She owed money at the site shop where the tenants were forced to buy their paraffin at inflated prices, and, though the Assistance Board was making her an allowance, she was so deeply in debt that there was no possibility of getting straight. 'Not in this old world,' Elsie would say, beginning a sigh that ended in a cough and lighting another cigarette. 'You lose heart, you really do, what with one thing and another.'

Like all reformers – and perhaps we are right – I blamed her inertia on her circumstances. They were bad enough to excuse almost anything. Her caravan was at the worst end of the site, surrounded by a sea of mud whenever it rained, and close to the rubbish dump. Her boys were always in the throes of what she euphemistically called summer colic. The healthiest creatures on the site were the rats.

I urged her to go to the Council and complain. She agreed she should go, but of course she did not. She was not only too apathetic but also too afraid: the Council were mixed up, in her mind, with the police and the Government.

My duty seemed clear. If my aunts' upbringing had prepared me for anything, it was for just this sort of agitation. I went to Council meetings, asked questions from the gallery and wrote to the local press. I called on Labour Councillors: they agreed that the state of affairs on the site was shocking. I continued to call and they said they had the matter in hand, but I must be patient and understand that the pressure of business was overwhelming. I made a great nuisance of myself and, in the end, they resorted to the traditional method of dealing with trouble-makers: they asked me to stand for my own ward at the next local government elections.

That I got in – which had not been expected since this was a staunchly Conservative area – was due to two reasons. One was that all people knew about me was that I was making trouble about the caravan site and a lot of them assumed that because it was at the bottom of my own garden, I must naturally be on 'their side', whatever my political colour: that is, I wanted the site disbanded. The other reason was that a paternity suit had recently been brought against my opponent by one of the Council office cleaners, which caused a great deal of moral indignation – not so much on the poor woman's behalf, I'm afraid, as because it was felt he had 'lowered himself'. And in fact, though perhaps it is shocking to admit it, we took some advantage of this dreadful argument during the campaign: we said we did not want to bring personalities into the election, but of course it was important that members of the Council should be responsible people who would not take advantage of their 'special position'.

Richard was disgusted. He said he had always known politics was a dirty game and he could not understand how I could endure it. I thought this a stupid attitude, rather as if people sitting comfortably in a first-class railway carriage should complain that being an engine driver was a filthy occupation.

Once on the Council, I set out to persuade them to apply for a compulsory purchase order on the site, which could have been done before, of course, if anyone had been single-minded enough about it.

I was occupied several evenings a week. I was afraid Richard would mind, but, as it turned out, my election had happened at a convenient time. He had recently been appointed Deputy Head in a big, new, comprehensive school in South London, and his evenings were taken up with meetings and an occasional television programme: the comprehensive principle was attracting a lot of public interest and Richard was good at arguing and putting a case, besides looking very handsome on the screen. Since he was often late home anyway, I did not have to feel guilty about him.

My family seemed charming to me. I even enjoyed Nonni's company; when I came home in the evenings, she would make tea and we would discuss Tom and Oliver, their beauty, their brains, their marvellous futures. I was never tired now; all my old energy seemed to have returned. I took on additional work in the Council, bullying them to set up a committee to draft out statutory requirements for caravan sites – which later became the basis for a Private Member's Bill – and still had time to dig the vegetable garden and walk miles with the children, just for the pleasure of it.

This happy period of my life came to an end in rather a stupid way. At least, the occasion was stupid.

One evening in June, I took Tom down to the river after supper. He should have been in bed, but it was breathlessly hot, and Richard, who was at home, had been irritated by his whining. I thought that if I took him down to paddle for a while, it would cool him down and distract him, so he would be able to sleep.

Everyone on the site seemed to be out of doors, pottering round their tiny gardens, or lolling on the parched grass. Several people nodded and smiled at me as I went past, so I had no inkling of what was going to happen. Elsie joined me on the river bank and asked if it was hot enough for me.

After that she said nothing for a while, only sat watching me in a broody way. I thought she was probably going to ask for money. I didn't mind giving her money, but I remember I was ridiculously annoyed at the thought of the way she would put it. Could I spare her a bob or two to the end of the week? As if she ever paid it back! I suppose the heat had made me edgy: though I knew that to ask for money as a loan was the only way she could keep her dignity, I held an angry conversation with her in my mind.

But it wasn't money. She said, 'You know, they say you've done the dirty on us in the Council.'

I asked her what she meant.

'Oh come off it. You know, don't you?' She looked at me slyly and then sighed. 'Well, you know this purchase order you've got? They're only buying the site so they can clear out the caravans, aren't they? They're going to turn it into a recreation ground.'

'Don't be daft. You know that's not true.'

'You calling me a liar?'

'No. I just mean people are always getting hold of the wrong end of the stick.'

She said stubbornly, 'Well, there's some families got notice to quit this morning.'

'But they had a letter explaining why. Did you know that?'

She shook her head disbelievingly and I explained the Council's plan which was to shift one or two caravans – and re-house the families in them – but only so there would be room to make a decent road into the plot. There was an opaque look in her eyes. 'Well, don't go on at me, I'm just telling you for your own sake. It's all over the site, everyone's fed up, I can tell you. I don't know how you have the nerve to come down here, really. I'd be scared with the kid and all.'

She was warning me, I slowly realized. I gave an exasperated, schoolmarm's laugh. 'Don't be silly, Elsie.'

She shrugged her thin shoulders and got up, brushing the cigarette ash from her skirt. 'Silly or not, I'd bugger off while I had the chance,' she said and glanced over her shoulder.

I looked in the same direction and saw a group of men standing and staring at us. Elsie muttered something I couldn't catch and walked off, skirting the group, towards the far end of the site and her own caravan. One of the men shouted after her and she broke into an awkward trot. There was a burst of incomprehensible laughter. Then they turned back and looked at me.

I called Tom. I didn't think anything would happen, but it was so sultry: tempers rose in this weather. He came reluctantly, hanging back when I took his hand. He was pale with exhaustion and there were blue marks under his eyes.

We had to pass right by the men. No one spoke as we approached them, but as soon as we had gone by, a voice said, 'How'd you like to be turned out of your home, Missus?'

I turned too late to see who had spoken. Their faces were blank and sullen.

I said, 'No one's going to turn you out.'

They stood and looked at me. 'No one's going to turn you out,' mimicked a high, squeaky voice.

I felt myself shake with anger. I said, as calmly as I could, 'Don't be stupid. If anyone's told you . . .'

'Don't be stupid, don't be stupid,' squealed the mimic. He wasn't a man, only a big, overgrown boy, and he looked quite crazy and terrifying. They all did. There was no point in arguing.

I said that if any of them would like to come and see me at home, I would explain exactly what was happening. My legs had begun to tremble, with fear now, not anger. I squeezed Tom's hand to comfort both of us and began to walk away.

A lump of mud flew over our heads and exploded in front of me. I knew I should ignore it and walk on, but I was too furiously angry. I wheeled round to face them and a lump of earth hit me full in the mouth and another in my chest, half-winding me. I had enough breath left to shout that they should be ashamed of themselves, spitting out the dirt from my mouth, and working myself up into a state of high, excited indignation. Then Tom gave a shriek beside me. I looked down and saw there was blood on his forehead. He must have been hit by a stone.

I picked him up and stumbled over the rough ground to

the back gate of our garden, which was only about twenty yards away. No one followed us. When I glanced back as I opened the gate, they were standing still, in a discomfited little group: they had not meant, I suppose, to hurt the child.

'They didn't mean to hurt poor Tom, it was just a silly old accident,' I said, partly to comfort the child and partly to prevent Richard making an angry scene in front of him. He had barely answered when I explained what had happened. Now he was standing beside the sink while I bathed Tom's forehead, his face a mask of red, pent-up rage.

The cut was nothing. It stopped bleeding almost at once and Tom's sobs quietened. I gave him to Nonni who was clucking round the kitchen and said I must go and clean myself up. If Richard wanted to work off his consternation on me, it would be better if we were alone.

'This is the end,' he said, as soon as we were out of the kitchen. 'This is really the end.'

His hollow tone and his ridiculously red, swollen up appearance, made me laugh.

'Oh, my dear *God*,' he cried, and followed me into the bathroom, abusing me. This would be all over the town, whatever had I been thinking of, going down to the site, hadn't I any sense?

'I couldn't have known what would happen, could I?' I said reasonably. 'No one would think people could be so stupid. . . .'

But Richard was beyond reason. 'You never *think*, that's your trouble. You never think of anyone but yourself. Bone-selfish. As if it wasn't enough to neglect your husband and children, you get yourself involved in vulgar brawls. Tom too. How d'you think *he'll* remember this evening? Oh, I don't matter – I'm nothing, nobody, just the bloody fool who keeps a roof over your head – but I'd have thought you'd have the decency not to drag Tom into it. . . .'

'As if I meant to! You're being ridiculous. What *is* this all about? You're not neglected.'

I was near tears. *I* was the one who had been attacked, not Richard.

'Really? D'you really think I'm not? Maybe you do – you're so wrapped up in your rotten selfishness that you can't see anyone else.' He was looking at me as if he really hated me; he seized me by the shoulders and pushed me over to the bathroom mirror. 'Look at you, *look at you*.'

I hardly recognized my face. Apart from the dirt, it had got so thin. My eyes blazed out of this thin, dirty face, so large and angry.

'I look a bit of a hag,' I said, trying to make him laugh.

He dropped his hands from my shoulders and said bitterly, 'You said it, not me. D'you think you're fun to come home to? When you're *there* to come home to. Out night after night.'

'But so are you,' I protested, really astonished because he had been so reasonable about my activities up to now.

'And why? I don't come home because there's nothing to come home for, that's why. No wife. Not even a decent bloody *housekeeper*. Look at the meals we have, when Nonni doesn't cook them. *I* wouldn't give them to a dog. And look at my shoes! I haven't got a single pair of bloody shoes without holes in them.'

And he actually sat down on the edge of the bath and pulled off his right shoe and thrust it under my nose. There was a worn patch in the sole. He glared at me, quite beside himself with rage, and the whole scene seemed so absurd and nothing to do with anything that had really happened, that I began to laugh in a wild, helpless way, snorting through my nose.

He stood up and advanced on me. For a moment, I thought he was going to hit me with the shoe; then he dropped it on the floor and began to pull at my clothes. I protested, but only weakly; I was hysterical, and, I suppose, rather excited too: even when he had me down on the floor, jammed in an uncomfortable position with my head stuck between the pedestal of the wash basin and a slimy floor cloth someone

80

had left lying against the wall, I could still do nothing but laugh.

From the bathroom door, Tom let out a wail. 'Daddy's hurting Mummy,' he shouted, and we heard his descending sobs as he ran down the stairs to Nonni. Richard stood up at once, pulled his clothes straight, and held out his hand to me.

I was still laughing. Perhaps it was that, or frustration, or, more probable still, a queer kind of prudery – he would rather his mother thought him a brute than realize what we had been up to – that made him hit me. He struck me hard across the mouth so that my head cracked back against the bathroom wall.

It made my head swim, so that I can remember, after that, only hopeless confusion: Nonni coming in and crying, Richard yelling at her to get out and mind her own business, and behind it all, poor Tom sobbing and sobbing. The sound rang in my ears long after he had fallen asleep: when Richard sat beside me as I lay on our bed, I thought I could still hear him through the wall.

Richard said he was sorry. 'I don't know what it was – I was so scared when you came in, all that blood and dirt. And I suppose I have been resentful, all these months. I felt as if I didn't exist for you.'

I said, coldly and pompously – he had put me in such a strong, moral position by hitting me – that if he really felt I was such an awful wife, if would be better if we got a divorce.

This scared him, as I knew it would. He is terrified of divorce because of his own childhood. He grabbed at my hands and held them to his chest and begged me not to say such a thing. He was so sorry, it was all his fault. I was a marvellous wife and he was proud of me, he didn't care what I did – I could become Lord Mayor of London for all he cared – only I must never leave him.

He looked distraught, on the edge of tears, and I was

ashamed at once, because I had only suggested divorce to punish him.

I said, 'I don't want to be Lord Mayor of London. I don't want to do something just for the sake of it, I don't really care about being on the Council, it's just that I wanted to do something about those wretched caravans. Poor Elsie. . . .'

I went on, telling him how pitiful her situation was, if he would only go and see he would understand, and how I felt it my duty to do what I could, working myself up into a noble sweat of righteousness. But all the time – from the moment I began to speak, in fact – I knew this was partly a lie: I enjoyed the intrigue of politics, the excitement, the feeling, if only in a limited way, of power. And as soon as I had admitted this, it suddenly seemed despicable to me.

Richard said, carrying on his own monologue as though I hadn't spoken. 'I know I shouldn't have minded, you've a right to your own life, it's just that – well, you never come up to London in the evenings, you're always too busy. I know that and I do understand why, but one thing leads to another, you know how it is. I mean, one doesn't *want* to get involved with other people. . . .'

He was looking at me in a desperate way. It may seem stupid, but it wasn't until years later, when we were in Morocco, that I understood what he was trying to tell me then. It wasn't that I wasn't listening, I heard him all right; but I was busy with my own thoughts, or, rather, my own feelings – the two were inextricably mixed together at this moment – and what he said was merely a background to the tumult that was going on inside me.

I looked at Richard. He seemed like a different person, much older, worn and harried. I thought that his appearance meant he had really been suffering very much, longing for me to give up my work, and had only refrained from asking me to do so out of respect for my 'rights'. This moved me deeply. How could I have been so irresponsible, putting my foolish ambitions before Richard and my children? And how petty those ambitions were, really, besides my family's happiness. Richard was right: I had not, at any point, thought of them, only of myself. My concern about the caravan site was only a kind of self-importance, and, as a result of my terrible selfishness poor Tom had been frightened in a way that might well scar him for much longer than that little stone. Poor Tom, my poor, poor baby. I hadn't wanted him before he was born, and, though I had never neglected him physically, I hadn't loved him in the way most mothers love their children. I remembered how Sophie had kissed and cuddled her babies. I had never been able to do that, not with such unselfconscious pleasure, perhaps because deep down I had resented his existence which was preventing me doing all the marvellous things I had intended to do in the world. Tom was to suffer, through no fault of his own, for a silly girl's anger at being 'tied down'. He had been late talking – was that because I hadn't coo-ed at him and gurgled baby talk? And what were my wonderful talents, that I should have felt it mattered that they were 'wasted'?

It was like a revelation.

I said, 'I'm going to give it up.'

He must have thought I meant our marriage, I see now. After what he had told me, or thought he had told me, it must have seemed reasonable. He threw himself down on the bed with his head on my stomach, groaning, and between the groans saying that he would be a good husband in future, he honestly would, he adored me, he was very ashamed and only hoped I could forgive him. I was surprised at the violence of his remorse – after all, he had only hit me – and I remember thinking, quite irrelevantly, how much more true to life the old dramatists were than modern ones, making their characters utter loud cries and throw themselves about the stage in moments of anguish, rather than deliver their parts poker-faced, through stiff lips.

I said, 'It doesn't matter – heaven's above, you didn't *hurt* me. But I've made up my mind. I shall resign from the Council. It isn't fair to anyone. Not to you, or the children.' All the time, I was straining my ears to hear Tom through the wall. 'If I keep on with it, I shall end up by doing nothing well. You can't run two lives properly. You were right to say I'd neglected you. I've been horribly selfish.'

Richard was looking at me. He seemed to be holding his breath. Then he kissed me and said, 'Well, as to that, you'll have to make up your own mind. I'm not going to persuade you, one way or another.'

'Darling, I have made up my mind,' I said.

He kissed me again and went out of the room, saying he thought it would be a good idea if he got us a drink. I lay on the bed, peacefully at one with myself. Earlier I had felt as if I was being torn in two, but now the decision was made, I was floating on a warm tide of physical ease, as if I had just given birth. I would devote myself in future to my family. I would not let them suffer from my selfish desire to have my own life. My life belonged to them; my duty was clear.

I was, of course, very stupid. Because, apart from the emotion of the moment, what had made me take this decision was really a kind of pride: I had to see myself as someone who had done the 'right thing'. I was, simply, not prepared to go on with the discomfort of feeling – or knowing other people might feel – that I was in any way neglecting my family. Nor could I face, any longer, the shame of admitting I wanted a life of my own, in case this should lay me open to a charge of pretentiousness or self-importance.

Perhaps I might have recognized my own hypocrisy, if it had not been for Richard's behaviour in the next months. He brought me flowers, took me out to dinner and the theatre, and was generally attentive to me, as if I were his mistress and not an old married woman. If, at any point, I thought that his solicitude was the sort of tender kindness you might show to someone utterly dependent and helpless – a prisoner or a caged bird – I was ashamed at once and re-doubled my efforts to be a good wife, asking Nonni to teach me how to cook the elaborate dishes Richard liked, and taking care to change my dress before he came home in the evening.

Chapter Eleven

'It's a man's world,' Flora said.

Richard was in bed with dysentery. Flora and I were walking through the palm grove, on mud paths between tiny squares of pale green barley. A flock of little boys followed us, chattering in a mixture of Arab and French. The girls, Flora explained, were all at home, working.

'Though whether women really have a worse time in this sort of society is a matter for argument,' she said. 'In some Berber tribes, their legal rights aren't as limited as one might suppose. Divorce, for example, often takes place on the initiative of the wife. And at least, what rights they have got are clearly defined and acted upon. At home, women may have all the rights they could want on paper, but they often vanish in a cloud of prejudice when you try to put them into practice! Look how difficult it is for women to get on in the medical or legal profession! And there's another point I think I shall bring out in my book. Here in North Africa, as I've told you before, it's the richer classes who shut up their women – the poor can't afford to. Whereas with us, it's the young, working-class housewife who suffers most from isolation. She's totally cut off from other adults during the day, and when her husband comes home in the evening, all he wants is telly and early bed. . . .'

I wondered if she really felt strongly about this or if it was just a habit to sound as if she did. She is, after all, paid to feel strongly, to produce definite-sounding opinions on this and that. 'You could say that a great many English women are still metaphorically wearing the yashmak,' she said now, speaking with a kind of didactic, impersonal severity, as if I were a studio audience.

I refrained from saying that it would never occur to me to make such a remark. 'You could, I suppose, but only as a sort of game. I know there's an *attitude* at home – men are people but women are only women – but that's not the same things as putting your women in purdah.'

'I don't think it's just an attitude. I know people – intelligent people – who send their sons to universities and their daughters to secretarial colleges.'

We passed a clump of eucalyptus trees that smelt of tom cats. I thought: if Richard and I had a daughter, would we quarrel over this?

'Usually it's just meanness, isn't it, not principle?'

'They think they have an excuse to be mean, though. They can point to all those young married women with degrees who sit at home and grumble.'

'Young men must grumble about dead-end jobs too. Only we don't hear so much about it.'

'But no one tells them they *ought* to be in this dead-end job and *liking* it.'

'Home knits are best for Baby and such fun to do.'

'Cooking is creative. Whip up this delicious sweet in five minutes and see Hubby's eyes sparkle.'

Flora's laugh hollowed her cheeks and made her almost beautiful. I thought: why should I laugh with her?

'It's hard on men, too. It can't be much fun, catching the same train every morning to the same dull job.'

Flora pulled a face. She wouldn't know anyone, man or woman, in a dull job. She walked ahead of me on the narrow path; she had slender legs and pretty ankles. A little boy tugged at my skirt; I looked down and saw a brown face with the sun on it, smiling.

'Someone has to look after the children.'

Flora waved her hand impatiently. I knew what she meant. All that can be arranged, once you want to, and anyway, having babies was behind us now, an old-fashioned activity. 'It's the small things that matter,' she said. She was wearing a blue shift that made her arms and legs look very brown. As she turned to wait for me at the end of the path, I felt I was looking at her for the first time: her face paler than her arms, a blonde shadow on her upper lip, no lipstick.

She looked at me with a reflective, appraising look. I was frightened by her. I wished I had some small thing to show her as a reference: perhaps not a book, an article in a learned journal. Scandinavia for the Eighteenth Century Reader. Abnormalities of human chromosomes following therapeutic irradiation. These titles came into my head from nowhere. *Elizabeth is really THE expert on abnormalities of the chromosomes. You would never guess it, she is so modest, but she knows more than anyone else in England on how the eighteenth century reader regarded Scandinavia....*

Flora said, 'My first husband used to separate the men from the women at the end of dinner.'

'Why did you put up with it?'

'I suppose I thought it was rather grand, playing at ladies and gentlemen.'

She was trying to be friendly, to show me that she, too, could be human and silly.

'Was that why you left him?'

She shook her head and put her dark glasses on. 'He got impotent. After I began to earn more money than he did. He said it un-manned him.'

'How extraordinary.' I gave my awful, loud laugh.

'It wasn't just that. We were unsuited temperamentally. It was all quite amicable in the end – until he took all the furniture, that is. The flat was mine, you see, but he'd bought the furniture, so he took everything except the child's cot. He only left that because she was sleeping in it. He took the light bulbs, too. He left Lalage and a packet of candles. That was gentlemanly, I suppose.'

I was embarrassed by these revelations. 'Lalage's a pretty name.'

'Of course, from his point of view, it was understandable. He'd been betrayed sexually, why should he leave me with anything?'

'Did he mind about Lalage?'

'Only as a weapon against me. And only until he got married again. He had a girl friend who got pregnant – he was only impotent with *me* – and she assumed marriage was the answer.'

'It must have been an awful time for you.'

'Not really. It was a relief, once he'd gone. He was a jealous person – where have you been, what have you been doing? I can't bear jealous people.'

'I suppose it showed he cared about you.'

'Only on a very low level, as a possession.'

We walked past a man making a mud wall between two wooden planks, pouring in the mud and banging it down. We came on to the dirt road and a woman in a fluttering robe of pale pink organza walked towards us. She had silver bracelets on her plump arms. I thought: who are these people? Who am I? We should mean something to each other, something more than animated objects, walking. But I could only feel the sun on the back of my head and a sad, frightened sensation, as if something inside me was crying.

'Is Richard a jealous man?'

'He's not really had much cause.'

'Are *you* jealous?'

'I've not had much cause, either.' What does she want to know?

'Oh *duckie*. With his looks?'

'We lead a very quiet life, you know.' My fear increased. Suddenly I felt that if I explained this to her, it would make her safe, impotent, like taking out a fuse or the rotor arm. 'He works very hard and then there's the garden and the children and his mother and my old aunt. Two old ladies and two boys make a fairly engrossing household. And he likes the garden. I mean, he *really* likes it. He gets obsessed by things like greenfly on the roses.'

'I thought he was quieter than he used to be. Less *spring*. Is he beaten down, do you think?'

'Well, everyone gets older.'

It had happened behind our backs. Richard was the youngest man ever to be made Head of so large a school. That was a long time ago. There had been photographs in the paper, a small paragraph in the *Londoner's Diary*. I had been amazed. I suppose no young woman takes her husband's career seriously to begin with. The day Richard started teaching, he was so nervous he couldn't eat breakfast. Then, suddenly, he was this man in the newspaper, a successful face, somewhat heavier, looking confident, powerful.

'Do you think he was wise to stick to teaching? He could have had a career in journalism or on television.'

'I don't know that he wanted it. It was only in the beginning, when we needed money badly, when we had to spend a lot on the house.'

'People were very impressed with him, though.'

'What people?'

The evening storm was coming up. Huge, black clouds rushed on the horizon. The tops of the trees in the palm grove rustled beneath us as we walked up the road, round the earthern rampart to the hotel. Over the edge, I could see a shop in the street below, a single room like an open cave, where an old man with white hair stood behind a counter that held a pair of scales and boxes of eggs and seeds.

'Oh, people one knew.' Flora glanced at me, as if wondering whom I knew. 'Malcolm Muggeridge. Kingsley Martin.'

I thought: why do women always have to talk about the men they are interested in? Even to their wives. Does she think me so stupid that I don't know they do that? Or doesn't she care? I was suddenly terrified, as if from a long distance away I had seen my family poised on the edge of a crumbling cliff, unaware and smiling. I thought: Flora is dangerous because she isn't frightened.

'He never talked much about those things he did,' I said. 'They were just an extra chore to do before he came home.'

'Of course, he was always devoted to you,' Flora said.

*

I said, 'Did you know we were going to meet Flora in Morocco?'

Richard was still in bed. He rolled over, yawning artificially, rubbing his eyes.

'Why should you think I knew?'

'I don't. I asked you if you did.'

Above his blue pyjamas, the skin of his face was shiny and tight with too much sun. He pondered, as if over some deep, philosophical point. I thought: if he says no, I shan't believe him. I hoped he would say no.

'Well, not really. But I knew she was coming.'

I had a heart-stopping sensation of falling, as if in a dream. But I was standing, bare-foot, on the patterned linoleum of this room in Morocco. I have big, square feet; there was a corn on my left little toe.

'Why didn't you tell me?'

'It wasn't important.' He smiled boyishly, crinkling his eyes. I remembered a quarrel we had, driving home in our Morris Thousand from a dinner party in Highgate. What had it been about? Some girl he knew, a big, red-haired girl in a tight frock. 'So this is your elusive wife,' she said when we met, baring beautiful, smooth teeth smudged with pale lipstick. Richard had talked to her all evening. 'Oh, I'd seen her around,' he said, in the Morris. 'Some stupid party or other, all chat and standing up, the kind of thing you hate. Why should I tell you, you never ask? What does it matter, anyway? Someone I met at a party! It's not important.'

'When did she tell you she was coming?'

'Oh God – sometime or other.' His eyes met mine. He gave a mock groan. 'If you must have chapter and verse – you remember that piece I did for the *Statesman*? Well, she rang me up about it, we had a drink. There was some programme she wanted to do, but I couldn't do it, so we talked about our holidays. She said she was going to Morocco with Adam Springer. We were just chatting. That's all.'

'You knew we were going to be here at the same time?'

'I suppose so.' He grinned; pulling up his pyjama jacket

and scratching. Acting boredom. 'She said she'd probably be bored with young Adam by Fez.'

I thought: why not accept it? Isn't that what old married people do, to avoid trouble? We are really quite comfortable with each other. Why think about that time years ago? It's history. He would just stare and say, whatever do you want to drag that up for? Christ Almighty, I told you at the time, didn't I? It's all over and done with, not my fault if you didn't take it in then. . . .

Richard groaned, closing his eyes. Then he heaved himself up and went into the lavatory. He came out and flopped on to the bed. I sat beside him and he stroked my arm.

'It's getting better. That's the first time for a couple of hours. But it makes you feel so bloody weak.'

'Will you be all right to go on tomorrow?'

'Sure to be. Don't worry. You go and have a good dinner. Maybe I'll get up and join you.'

'Try and sleep first.'

He pulled the sheet up to his chin and stretched out obediently. I took off my clothes and went into the shower. There was a mirror on the wall and I stood and looked at myself. My body is still all right. There are a few pregnancy marks on my stomach, round the navel, but my legs are long and unveined. Not bad, really.

I put on the towelling bathrobe and went back into the bedroom. Richard was sleeping, his mouth slightly open. I thought: jealousy is an ugly emotion, mean, hideous. Why should I be jealous of Richard when I don't want to make love to him any more? It's only possessiveness, pride and fear. Fear of growing old, of dying alone.

He was sweating. He had a blanket over him, twisted up round his neck. I pulled it off gently, so as not to wake him, moistened a handkerchief with cologne and wiped his forehead.

He smiled in his sleep. I sat on the edge of the bed and wrote him a letter in my mind:

My dear Richard,

Let us be sensible and admit the truth. Our children are almost grown, they don't need us any more. Not as a unit. We have fulfilled our biological function. We have stopped breeding. That is only a part of life, and as it no longer concerns us, why should it hold us together? Does anything? People don't stop changing and growing just because they are married. We are quite different people now, we need different things. That's all – there's no need for closely reasoned complaints or long self-justifications. I know how you feel about divorce but isn't that an attitude that needs re-thinking? It was, anyway, only a reaction against childhood instability, valid while the children were small but not rational grounds now for two reasonable people to continue together. Of course we could leave things as they are and just go our own ways, but it wouldn't work. We aren't reasonable enough to accommodate ourselves to such a shift in moral attitudes. We could be free, or we could marry again, someone who suited the new people we have become. Of course this would be easier for you – a middle-aged man is more likely to find someone attractive than a middle-aged woman – but if I am prepared to accept this disadvantage, why should you grumble? I won't ask you to support me. You can keep the house, it's your house anyway, and you're fond of the garden. I would go right away, find a room somewhere and a job. It's time I supported myself. I might even enjoy doing it, so you need not feel any guilt about me. . . .

It was a good letter, if a little pompous. I began to cry. Richard stretched out his arm and pulled me down beside him. He said sleepily, 'It wasn't a deep laid plot. Honest, true. Matter of fact, I'd forgotten she was going to be in the bloody country until she turned up. I admit I remembered then, but I didn't tell you because it would have sounded daft that I hadn't told you before. As it seems it did.'

My nose was blocked with tears. I sat up and he gave me

the handkerchief out of his pyjama pocket. I blew. 'I must look hideous,' I said, relishing this.

'No more than usual.' He grinned amiably. 'You look to me very healthy and nice. But I'm afraid this stupid bug is hardly an aphrodisiac. Though I daresay you don't mind that.'

He looked at me questioningly. I wished I could say yes, I minded like hell, it wouldn't cost me much in the circumstances. But I am too honest – or too ungenerous: clamped tight like a mean smile or a poor woman's purse.

'It's a bit hot, really,' I said.

He sighed, not very deeply. He watched me, taking off my bathrobe. 'You've been bitten on your bottom. No, not there, the other side. Put some stuff on it.'

I took my clothes into the bathroom. I wanted to get dressed in private.

He called, through the open door, 'We can drop Flora as soon as we get to Marrakesh. I daresay we could now, there must be a bus or a car she could hire, but it seems a bit hard.'

'Don't be stupid.' I stalked back into the room and brushed my hair furiously, counting the strokes.

'I feel sorry for her, really.'

'Do you now?'

'Well. She feels – I think she feels – she's been a bright young woman long enough. She needs to do something concrete, make some sort of mark. That's why this book's important to her. She wants to do it but she's terrified at the same time. It's a kind of confrontation, you see. She's worrying about success and so on.'

'I'd have thought she was successful enough.'

'It probably looks all right from the bottom of the ladder. Balancing at the top – or near the top – is a trickier business.'

He spoke gloomily. I wondered if he was really talking about himself, but was too angry to ask. Why should I feel sorry for Flora? Don't we all have this inner uncertainty, this shivering core? Why should she get credit for it?

'She's had a pretty rotten time in some ways,' he said.

'Has she?'

He got out of bed and came behind me. In the mirror, his face glowered over my shoulder. 'Don't be a bitch, Elizabeth,' he said, and bit my ear, rather harder than was pleasant.

Richard joined us for dinner, though he ate cautiously. After a bottle of wine, Flora talked about her second divorce, continuing the next instalment of the afternoon serial. It was as if she was checking over her life, wondering where she had got to. I found it hard to believe that Flora could suffer like other people from minor humiliations, personal relationships.

Her parents had made trouble when she left Arthur Dove. 'I think the first time they'd felt they must accept an honest mistake. They were very restrained. The second was different. My mother wrote dreadful letters – I was surprised how hurt I was! As if I was about fourteen! She said *she'd* stuck it out with my father all these years, just for my sake. I'd had a stable home at the price of her martyrdom and this was how I'd repaid her. How could I do this to Lalage. She wrote, "You might just as well throw that poor child on the compost heap." She's a very keen gardener, my mother. . . .'

Flora laughed, but tears clung to the end of her pale lashes; she was a little drunk. 'And the ridiculous thing was, of course, that I couldn't bear to tell her about Lalage and Arthur. As if my *mother* was the child to be protected! Though she had no inhibitions about me. She wrote as if she'd hated me all my life.'

'Parents can be terrible to their children,' Richard said, and touched her hand lightly.

They discussed their mothers. I was out of this conversation. My mother was only a sad woman in an old photograph, younger then than I was now. After dinner I left them to shed their autobiographical burdens, and joined the Hobbs at their table in the bar.

Mrs Hobbs was better. Her colour had come back but it was as if something, some spark, had gone out of her. She treated me like a daughter, with affectionate pride, complimenting me on my dress and asking about my children. 'You don't look old enough to be the mother of two great big boys. Does she, Daddy?' She smiled, but her china-blue eyes were blank and frightened.

We talked of our plans. We were all going on to Ouerzzazate. Richard had promised Mr Hobbs we would drive in convoy in case their car broke down again. I hoped to go down to the desert at Zagora. 'Don't do that, dear, take my advice, you won't like it.' Mrs Hobbs's hands fluttered in front of her like small, helpless wings in a storm. 'I can't explain, but it gave me the most terrible feeling. You look out of your window and then the wind blows and the next time you look it's all different. It made me feel funny. As if I suddenly knew I couldn't be sure of anything any more.'

She looked haunted, as if by something just beyond her vision.

'You had one of your bad turns, my love,' Mr Hobbs said. He leaned back in his chair, watching her. Most of us were red and peeling from the sun: he had been burned golden. He looked, with his long, Norman face, like an illustration in a book on heraldry. He wore a gold watch on his wrist; fine, gold hairs curled over the white, nylon strap. 'You were ill, darling, and it frightened you.' He creaked forward in his cane chair and took her restless hand between his narrow ones.

'Perhaps that's all it was. I'm a silly billy,' she said.

This is what marriage should be, I thought: two people comforting each other in the dark. There's no need for love in the daylight. I ought to tell Richard this, and we won't leave each other.

I felt tears come into my eyes as they had into Flora's at dinner. I'm maudlin, I thought, a sentimental fool.

'You look a bit tired, dear,' Mrs Hobbs said. 'Is your poor tummy quite better? Why don't you get her a brandy, Daddy? I'm sure she'd like it.'

'Would she now?' He smiled, gently mocking.

'I'd love one,' I said.

He went to the bar. She looked after him and said, in a low voice, 'I wish I could tell you what it was like in the desert. I felt – it was as if I suddenly knew I was going to die and I was nothing, just sand and dust blowing away.' She looked at me with a sudden hope. 'I'm very ill, you know,' she said.

We discuss death sometimes, in a mature and balanced way. 'Once one has reached forty, one should have faced up to the fact of one's own death,' Richard says. We agree that everyone should be told if they have a mortal disease. We have promised to tell each other if the doctors refuse to. It is simply a matter of reasonable human dignity.

I said, 'Goodness me, if you were really ill, you could never have stood up to this trip the way you have. Travelling in this dreadful heat!'

The gleam of hope vanished. Had she really thought she could talk to me? I shrank from her eyes; they were like blind, blue flowers. 'That's what Daddy says. But I see him looking at me. I don't want him to worry, so I try to be bright and keep going.'

I said, brisk as a uniformed nurse, 'I'm quite sure you've nothing to worry about.'

She gave one of her little, puffing sighs. 'It's tiring to pretend all the time. When I was down there, in the desert, it didn't seem worth pretending any more.'

Chapter Twelve

At the time Suez happened, I was pregnant. I wanted this baby. Tom and Oliver were growing up, tough little boys in jeans with limp, mouse-coloured hair. I fed them plates of baked beans; squeezed oranges, bandaged knees, bowled cricket balls, ran beside tottering bicycles, read nonsense poems at bedtime, baked wholemeal bread, earthed up King Edward potatoes in the garden. When the boys were in bed, Richard and I had friends in: we ate supper in the kitchen, by candlelight. We all had young families; people without children seemed strange to us, beings from a forgotten world; we discussed education and the bomb. We were all serious in a cheerful way and very hard working, though none of the wives had jobs. Being a woman was a full-time occupation, they said.

I had kept my side of the bargain, my teetotaller's pledge. If sometimes, when I canvassed for other people at elections, addressed envelopes, drafted manifestoes, I felt like an alcoholic sneaking a secret drink, this was a purely subjective analogy. Richard approved of my having an 'interest' now it did not dominate my life and make his uncomfortable, and the fact that his political opinions were different from mine, made him feel tolerant and wise. He liked me to air my opinions in front of our friends, most of whom felt as he did: he said I looked so pretty when I got excited.

I cannot remember that I minded this. When we quarrelled, it was about other things: bills, who had left the lawn mower out in the rain, nothing important.

There seemed no cracks in our life. Or perhaps, for convenience, we pretended not to notice them.

We disagreed over Suez. We didn't discuss it. I ordered a newspaper which held the same viewpoint as my own and we sat, at breakfast, shielded by our own opinions, warily silent.

I went to a protest meeting at the Albert Hall. There was a great crowd, singing, shouting, all very good-humoured – not, I think, because they were taking the situation lightly but because they were buoyed up by the feeling that here was something quite above ordinary political argument, a clearly defined moral issue on which people could stand up and be counted.

As a result of this feeling there was a lot of high-spirited junketing. We cheered three Egyptians who stood up in the body of the hall and cried, 'We want Nasser'. We shouted, 'Reparations for Egypt', 'Eden must go', and sang the 'Red Flag'. During the singing, I glimpsed a familiar face and pushed my way through the crush, shouting '*William*'. He stared briefly and then became one enormous grin, pushing his spectacles up on his rubbery nose. For a moment he seemed quite dreadfully aged and the next I was used to him and he was quite unchanged. We had been at college together, always close, once a little in love. I felt I could weep with nostalgic affection. The crowd was very rough; we were jostled together. William clung to me, laughing. 'How *are* you, Elizabeth? How's Richard? Does he still bully you?'

William was one of the people Richard said had a second-class mind. I wondered if I should tell him this, and decided he might not think it funny.

'What sort of degree did you get?' I asked, and he looked surprised, as was perhaps reasonable: this was an odd question, after ten years. He didn't reply because there was a great crush at the exit, a group of young men with placards, shouting. We waited while policemen threaded their way through the crowd and hustled them away.

'What have you been doing?' William had been an engineer – or a biologist? I was ashamed not to remember.

'I'm a postman. Tele-communications. You don't want to know. Are you well? You look marvellous. Do you remember Rose Potter? I married her. Three boys.'

'I've got two.'

We shouted our biological achievements at each other as if nothing else mattered. The crowd was surging out of the hall, we were carried along with it and I was worried about the baby in all this pushing and shoving, but didn't like to mention it in case William should feel he had to take care of me.

We went to a coffee bar. When we were students, we had spent most of our time in cafés, arguing, holding hands.

'Dear Elizabeth, back in our natural habitat,' William said, and held my hand now. We were both uplifted, lit with pleasure and excitement, in each other, in the meeting. William said it was the best political occasion he could remember since he had heard Aneurin Bevan speak in South Wales during the war. William came from Aberdare. When I first knew him he had spoken with a beautiful, accented Welsh voice; now the lilt was gone and he talked flatly, like a Londoner.

But when he talked he looked the same as he had always done; eager, intent, screwing up his boneless nose, gesturing with broad, stubby-fingered hands. 'The country's split down the middle on this thing, you know, there's been nothing like it since *Munich*. And it's not a political division, either. You can go into a pub full of cloth caps and they're all shouting to put down the wogs. It's extraordinary – I know families who've stopped speaking to each other. My Dad – I couldn't have *believed* it! – we went down last weekend and he was sitting there, polishing the buttons on his old uniform and calling me a traitor!'

We capped each other's stories. It was a marvellous sort of excitement, like being young again. We talked until I missed the last train. He said he would drive me home. We weren't young; we were around thirty. I had a husband and two children; William had Rose Potter and three boys in Surbiton. We stopped the car somewhere near Richmond Park, off the main road; we smoked and watched the headlights go by. William wanted to make love to me; it wasn't a very determined attempt, friendly rather than passionate. I refused because I was afraid for the baby, though I didn't tell him that.

'It was just a thought, old dear,' he said. 'No offence meant.'

'None taken,' I said. 'Dear William.' He held my hand all the way home.

The house was dark except for a light in the kitchen. Nonni was waiting up, reading the racing page of the evening newspaper. 'Poor Richard was worried,' she said, looking over the top of her spectacles.

'He's gone to bed, though?'

'Oh yes. He can't afford to miss his sleep. I'll make you some chocolate.'

I told her about the meeting. A flush rose up in her cheeks.

'It's disgusting,' she said. 'Disgusting. A lot of dirty traitors.'

I stared at her. I had not thought she was sufficiently interested to take sides one way or the other. She got up and began walking round the kitchen, collecting a dirty cup here, a saucer there, putting them in the sink. 'I told Richard I'd say nothing to you, but I can't keep silent,' she said, 'it's not fair to ask me.'

'Of course not.' My head was swimming and I felt very tired suddenly. 'Of course you must say what you think, everyone must.'

'You won't like it, though. Oh, I know what your opinions are, they're different from mine and Richard's, but people are entitled to think differently if they want to, I've never said anything else. But this is something else again, having socialist ideas is one thing, betraying your country another, people who do that have no rights at all, that's my opinion, they ought to be just put up against a wall and shot. Though shooting's too good for them, if you ask me, we're too soft in this country, we could do with a bit of Hitler here I think sometimes instead of the namby-pamby way we go on. . . .' She turned the tap on, and the plumbing clanged.

'But that's ridiculous,' I said, trying to speak lightly and reasonably, trying to smile. 'You *can't* think like that – and, anyway, since we're not at war with Egypt, no one's a traitor. People who think like me are simply protesting against the Government's action in a perfectly legitimate way – we think they're wrong to attack Egypt and we want to stop them before any further damage is done. It's the only way. . . .'

She turned round. Her face had got rounder as she had grown older; in her spectacles, she looked like an angry owl.

'Oh, don't tell me, there's no need. I know what your lot think, it makes me sick.'

'Oh, Nonni . . .' I felt a throb of excitement – or fear. At the back of my mind was a small, warning voice, telling me it was ridiculous to go on with this, that I couldn't change Nonni's mind, nor would it alter anything if I could.

'You want us to give up everything,' she said, 'all our rights, our place in the world. You're ashamed to be decent English people, you want us to go crawling and grovelling. . . .'

Reason vanished. All at once, I was in a wild fury of rage: I saw, not Nonni, but all the foolish and ignorant people who seemed at this moment to be conspiring together against all the forces of right and reason to poison and destroy the world.

'But it's *not* decent to go to war over something like this,' I screamed, thumping my fist on the table so that the cups on the dresser rattled. 'You're a stupid, ignorant woman, you think with your *bowels*, not with your head.'

'Don't you talk in that disgusting way to me, keep it for your clever friends who're trying to turn this fine country into a nest of crawling, grovelling, filthy snakes.'

'Don't be so *obscenely* stupid.'

'Using filthy words, that's typical. Using filthy words, forgetting our fine heritage . . . !'

'Rubbish, rubbish, *rubbish*,' I yelled. I felt as if the top of my head was lifting off.

'Spitting,' she shouted. '*Spitting* on the grave of the Unknown Warrior. . . .'

'Christ, what's going on?' Richard stood in the doorway in his pyjamas. 'For God's sake, Elizabeth, if you must go rushing off to protest meetings, couldn't you have done your protesting *there*, and let the rest of us sleep in peace?'

His querulous tone provoked me. It seemed shocking that he should feel he had a right to complain about being woken up when the country was on the verge of civil war.

'Your bloody *mother*,' I moaned. I was frightened by the helpless, shaking anger that had hold of me; I wanted to get out of the room. Moving round the table, I jabbed myself painfully on its corner, and burst into tears.

'Oh, Nonni. . . .' Richard said, still sounding no more than irritated, and a trifle superior, like someone who has been held up on his way home by a street brawl. 'Oh Lord – I did ask you. Couldn't you have kept quiet?'

She was trembling, her mouth was working; she looked old and humiliated. 'It's more than flesh and blood can stand, listening to that Communist ranting.'

'*Communist*. You're a Fascist. A murdering Fascist,' I cried and Richard took me gently by the shoulders and pushed me towards the door. 'Go on, up to bed, I'll settle this. . . .'

I felt exhausted: as I dragged myself up the stairs I can remember thinking that now I knew what people meant when they said they were 'tired to death'. I fumbled out of my dress and crawled into bed in my underclothes. My heart was thumping as if I had run a race and there was a pain in my back.

Richard came in. He sat on the end of the bed in the moonlight and put his head in his hands. A little later, he said, 'Will you go and apologize? She says she's leaving. I can't do anything.'

The injustice of this request seemed so intolerable that I couldn't speak.

He waited a minute. Then he said, 'It's nothing to do with what's right or wrong, just that she's old and she's got nowhere to go.'

I got slowly out of bed. I felt a fearful indignation, like heartburn. My hands and feet were very cold. It was an effort to reach up for my dressing-gown which was hanging on the back of the door and I felt bitter against Richard because he didn't see that I was ill and come to help me. I put my gown on, taking as long as I could, and walked slowly down the passage to Nonni's room.

She had her suitcase open on the bed and was muttering to herself as she took clothes out of drawers and threw them in. Her hands were shaking so much that she kept dropping things on the floor. She didn't look up when I said I was sorry I had been unkind, just went on opening drawers and dropping things and muttering; I had begun to wonder if she had heard me, when she said, 'All right, all right, I'm going just as soon as I can get my things together, I'm not one to stay where I'm not wanted.'

'But I do want you, Nonni,' I said. 'Please believe me. I'm so sorry, I shouldn't have said the things I did.'

She took no notice, and I began to hate her, not because I was having to apologize – she looked so old and sad that I was genuinely sorry – but because she wouldn't listen and it was such a terrible physical struggle for me to talk; my mouth seemed to be full of some sickly, sticky stuff, like chewing-gum. I realized that in fact she was absolutely determined on going, she hadn't the imagination to act out this sort of scene to punish me, nor, to be fair, would she ever have been so spiteful if she had. I felt helpless and despairing and suddenly so ill that I had to clutch at the door to stop myself falling. I must have moaned: she looked at me coldly as if suspecting some kind of trickery, and then her face altered and she came across the room to take my arm and help me back to bed.

Chapter Thirteen

Of course everyone – except, I suppose, Aunt Kit – thought that I left Richard because I was half out of my mind with distress at losing the baby, but this is not the truth, not the whole truth, anyway.

It is hard to remember, unless something similar is happening at the time, exactly how strongly people feel at moments of great political crisis, how they are carried away by conviction of the rightness of their own side and by contempt and hatred of the other. It seemed that the Suez crisis marked a point of no return, not only for the country, but also for Richard and me. People of opposing political views can live together, as can people of different religions, until something happens to make them meet head-on, and then one of them must give way. And neither of us would.

There is no torment like knowing you are absolutely, morally right over something of immense importance and being unable to convince someone else of it. I lay in bed and ranted at Richard; explaining, arguing, weeping with frustration. Richard would not budge an inch: I began to think he must be mad or wicked – or both.

I should explain that I never once thought that he should 'give way to me' – as Nonni said he should – because I was ill; only because, as I told him, I had always thought of him as 'a reasonable human being with some pretensions to morality'. My fervour was religious: I fought to save his sinner's soul as ardently as any missionizing Christian.

And when he said that he couldn't agree with me, but please, please couldn't we let the matter drop since nothing we said or did could alter the course of events, I was enraged because it seemed to me that this really *was* his attitude, he wanted a quiet life, not to be involved. 'You are like Pontius Pilate,' I shouted at him. 'A moral vacuum.'

It took me three days to decide that our life together was impossible. We were totally unsuited: there was no point in pretending any longer. The children were staying with a neighbour; in the afternoon, Nonni went shopping. She was away a long time. I lay and thought of her, trying on corsets while the world fell to pieces. I got out of bed, packed a suitcase, wrote a note for Richard saying I was leaving him, and walked to the station.

My aunts lived not much more than thirty miles away, but it was an awkward, cross-country journey. I had to take two trains and a bus; by the time I got there I was bleeding badly, giddy and incoherent with exhaustion. But I suppose I must have told them how things were between me and Richard because as I lay on my bed, in my old room, I heard Aunt Lilian telephoning.

'No,' she said. 'No, you'd better not come. Yes. Yes, of course I'll let you know.'

I slept. I felt as if I were drowning in sleep. My heart stopped thumping. Aunt Lilian said I was thin and ordered two extra pints of milk a day. They bought a lot of milk, anyway; the larder was full of it, poured into china jugs and covered with muslin veils weighted with coloured beads. Apart from milk, they seemed to live largely on bread and baked beans. They peeled no vegetables, roasted no joints, bought no floor polish or detergent, no furniture cleaner or disinfectant. The house was dusty but restful. We sat by the fire, listened to the news on the radio and ate baked beans. We did not discuss Richard, only the Government's action and the terrible news from Hungary. I began to feel, as I had always felt with my aunts, that personal affairs were unimportant: we were only sticks in the great river of history that was sweeping us along.

I had not seen them for some time. Aunt Lilian had got very thin: her skin seemed to hang on her, like a shapeless dress. I thought she was quieter than I remembered, but perhaps that was because Aunt Kit had become so much more talkative. Aunt Kit passed her days in a routine of 'little nips' of brandy, chain-smoking, listening to the news and hiding money. She hid it under cushions, in vases, under the stair carpet, and then forgot where she had put it. Apart from this minor eccentricity – and I knew old people often became eccentric – she seemed to me the same as she had always been: vague in practical matters but sharp-witted enough in other ways, and eager to talk about what was happening in the world.

One afternoon, when Aunt Lilian was lying down, I told Aunt Kit that Richard was on the 'other side' over Suez and that I had decided to leave him. She took it calmly. 'You should never have married a Tory,' she said. 'Oil and water don't mix. You must get the boys away before they are tainted.'

The state I was in, this seemed a perfectly sensible remark. We began to discuss what should be done and how I would manage to support the children, and if, from time to time, I had the feeling that something was wrong, it was only in a distant, elusive way, as if I was listening to someone playing a piano on the other side of the road and hearing occasionally, but only occasionally, a wrong note. Aunt Kit said that the best thing I could do initially was to train as a teacher. Later on, perhaps at the next election, there might be an opportunity for me to get into Parliament. It was unlikely that I would be offered a safe seat, but I might, with luck, be given a chance in a marginal. 'I've still got some influence you know, dear. I may have been out of the arena for a while, but I daresay there are still some who remember the old gladiator.'

Her eyes misted at this heroic image, and she poured herself a brandy. She was wearing a man's woollen dressing-gown: the sleeves were too long for her and although she kept rolling them up, they fell down again almost immediately, shedding a little, grey storm of cigarette ash. I realized, suddenly, that I hadn't once seen her properly dressed since my arrival. 'Still, that's in the future,' she said. 'I daresay this knavish lot will be in power for a long time yet. We have to plan for the future. Eyes on the stars and feet on the ground.'

There was a school for the boys at the end of the road. We could turn out the attic and make a nursery for them. She drained her glass and insisted that we go up at once and inspect the top floor of the house.

The attics were full of papers: suitcases of Fabian pamphlets, old party manifestoes, notices of meetings, printed Chatham House lectures, back numbers of *The Times*, *The Guardian*, *The Spectator*, the *New Statesman*. Aunt Kit sat down on a tin trunk, rolled up the sleeves of her gown, and looked at me. 'Are we going to play the Game, dear?' she said.

Aunt Lilian had invented the Game when I was at school in order to increase my knowledge of world events and give me a sense of history. While other families played Monopoly and Mah Jong, we sat round the fire, Sunday evenings after supper, and read out old leaders from *The Times* in turn. The skill lay in selecting them, so that the others would find it hard to guess the date and what they referred to.

'Shall I begin?' Aunt Kit said, and smiled at me.

Aunt Lilian appeared in the doorway. She said, 'What are you doing, Kit? If you smoke up here, you'll set fire to the house.'

Aunt Kit picked up a newspaper and smoothed it out on her knee. 'Elizabeth has left Richard,' she said. 'He believes Anthony Eden was right.'

Aunt Lilian looked at me. Then she said, very gently, 'Kit, why don't you go down now, and put the kettle on for tea? It's time, and the baker brought us a nice treat this morning.'

'Toasted buns?'

'Two each.'

Aunt Kit stood up. She looked round her with a surprised air. 'I'm cold,' she complained, 'I can't think why we came up here.'

When she had gone, Aunt Lilian said, 'Perhaps you'll tell me what this is about?'

I was shocked by the revelation of Aunt Kit's condition. I stumbled out that I couldn't live with Richard any longer.

Aunt Lilian waited. I said, 'There's no point in pretending. My life is *nothing*. I pretended I was happy, you can make yourself think anything, but I'm not.'

It had seemed quite clear when I was talking to Aunt Kit. I was making a mature and rational decision. Richard and I were totally unsuited, we cramped each other, preventing further growth, we were better apart. But Aunt Kit was mad. Was I?

'Has Richard been unfaithful to you?'

'I don't know. I don't care. He's got his life and I've got

nothing. *I'm* nothing. Just a pair of hands peeling potatoes and a reflection in the mirror. I don't *exist.*'

'In the eighteenth century, anatomists used to dissect bodies in search of the soul,' Aunt Lilian said. 'They never found it. What's troubling you is that, nothing to do with Richard.'

I began to cry. 'I want to leave him. You don't know what my life is like. I'm a housekeeper, a kind of serf – what I think doesn't matter, only whether the cheese *soufflé* rises and if there are buttons on his shirt. Wives don't count, you say they look pretty and bring them home bunches of flowers but you don't take them *seriously,* their tiny minds aren't capable of grasping anything important. You *know* what Richard thinks about Suez, but he doesn't really listen to me – how do you think that makes me feel?'

She paid this outburst close, if bewildered attention. Then, 'How does *he* feel, do you think? Rushing off to that meeting was almost certainly how you lost the baby. It was his baby too, have you thought of that?'

Her sudden vehemence stopped my tears like a slap in the face.

'He never said he minded.'

'Of course not. He's too decent to blame you. You have nothing but the silliest of complaints against him. If they are a sample of your usual conversation I'm not surprised that he doesn't listen to you. You're no more worth listening to than any bored, spoiled young woman, whining because the routine of married life has gone stale on you. It really is very provoking, to a woman of my generation. When I was thirty, we didn't have the vote, we had to fight for a place in the world. Now you've got it, most of you don't bother to use it. I daresay it's dull, being tied to a house and young children, but it was a life you chose, after all, you were so eager to rush into it that you didn't even take your degree.'

I wanted to tell her this wasn't quite true, that I had had no choice, but her grey, tired look stopped me: it would hurt her too much, I thought, to feel I had not trusted her with the truth in the beginning. I was – like Flora with her mother – in the stupid position of being unable to put the one argument that would have made her feel some sympathy for me.

All I could do was to mumble that I regretted not taking my degree, and, though I could see it was irritating of me to whine, to feel stale and bored was not such a trivial thing; that though we might have the vote now, meals still had to be prepared and children looked after and since this kind of drudgery was despised by society as not being 'real work', we were in the hideous position of being both exhausted and imprisoned by it and also looked down on for doing it; that I had honestly tried to be the sort of wife Richard wanted – and the sort of wife I felt I ought to be – but it was like being in a kind of airless cell and I could only see Richard as a jailer; that I saw myself becoming progressively more and more incapable of doing anything, not just mentally, but from some kind of paralysis of will.

She heard me out. She became very gentle – or perhaps she was only tired – and said, 'Well, dear, if you really feel you must leave him, of course we will do what we can to help you. I don't know how we will manage Tom and Oliver, Kit has her difficult days, you know, but we will do our best. And as to being incapable, good heavens you silly child, you have your life in front of you. . . .'

Richard came the next day, arriving at ten in the morning, when only Aunt Lilian was out of bed. I came down when she called me and found him standing in the living-room with a look of distaste on his face as he looked round at the overflowing ash trays, the dirty grate, the pile of chair cushions tumbled in the middle of the floor. As I came into the room, he changed his expression quickly and smiled at me.

'Have you been playing camps?' This was a game the boys played with the sofa cushions. I said no, it was just that before we went to bed last night, Aunt Kit had decided to look for her money.

He waited for me to go on, looking puzzled. When I was silent he came towards me, took my hands, and said with a formal air as if he had prepared this speech, 'I'm so sorry I upset you. Have you forgiven me?'

I could see he was going to be humble and it depressed me. People who apologize always put themselves so soundly in the right. I said, stiffly, that there was nothing to forgive.

'All right,' he said. 'Let's leave it at that. Are you coming home?'

I hesitated. Whether he guessed what I was likely to say I don't know, but he spoke with a sudden rush as if to prevent me from saying something that we would both have to accept and talk about.

'I love you, I really do, you know. That's all I care about – you and the children, my work a little, nothing else. And that's what you've got to consider – not duty or pity, or anything like that, because it doesn't really come into it, though you'll think it does. I *know* you,' he said, wisely smiling and crinkling up his eyes like an actor.

'Are you talking about the children?'

He shook his head. 'Nonni's had a stroke. She's not too bad, the doctor thinks she'll recover quite a lot of movement, though maybe not all. She's been asking for you, she feels terribly guilty about the baby.'

I felt suffocated. 'That wasn't her fault.'

'She thinks it was. She's torturing herself.'

'I'll go and pack now.'

'Are you sure? Don't you want to think about it?'

'No. I don't need to. I haven't any choice, have I?' *Don't be half-hearted, don't be a cold, half-hearted bitch.* 'I want to come home,' I said.

'Darling.' He kissed me. There were tears in his eyes.

I smiled. 'I won't be long. Go and talk to Aunt Lilian. I don't think she's well. I haven't really asked her, I've been too busy with myself. Try and find out if there's anything wrong, if you can.'

I went upstairs and put my suitcase on the bed and took

my things out of the drawers. I cried a little. For Nonni? For the baby? For my selfish freedom, my lovely freedom?

Elizabeth is a stupid, self-indulgent bitch, the inner voice said. I dried my eyes and went downstairs, smiling.

Chapter Fourteen

'I don't think I have ever taken a really big decision in my life,' Mr Hobbs said. 'I've always been – well – overtaken by events, you might say. My parents wanted me to be a school-master, but I married into the dry-cleaning business.'

We were driving down to Zagora. Mrs Hobbs had stayed behind in the hotel at Ouerzzazate because of the heat; Richard and Flora because there was to be a celebration for the King of the Belgians and Flora wanted to see the women dancing. The road to Zagora led over mountains, through a serrated, moon landscape. It was very hot. I couldn't remember how we had got into this conversation.

'And gave up teaching? That must have been a fairly im-portant decision.' He would have been a good schoolmaster, I thought: gentle, precise, dry-humoured.

'Not really. My father-in-law died and someone had to look after the business. Though Mrs Hobbs is a remarkable woman in many ways, she has no head for figures. And it wasn't you see, a matter of being intimately connected with other people's dirty clothes – that's something I was thankful for, I must admit. It was a thriving concern when I took over, so it was a mathematical problem, really. At least, that's how I saw it. Mathematics was my subject, I was simply trans-ferring what talents I had in that direction from one field to another.'

'Did you regret it?'

'Why should I?' He seemed genuinely surprised. 'My parents thought a schoolmaster's salary was riches, but they had always lived in very humble circumstances. Mrs Hobbs wasn't exactly accustomed to luxury, but the shoe had never pinched. She had lived a very gay life in London, when she was on the stage you know, and she had always had her parents behind her – like Pip, she had "Great Expectations". Naturally, I felt her comfort should be my first consideration. So the decision was made for me, you see, it was only afterwards that I saw I had taken quite a step – a leap in the dark, in fact. I might, after all, have made a mess of the whole thing. I can't think why it didn't occur to me at the time. It occurred to Mrs Hobbs, so she told me later, but she said nothing to me then. I admire her very much for that, you know. The whole of a small fortune might have gone down the drain, dribbled, you might say, through my inexperienced hands, but she never said a single word and the idea of failure never crossed my mind. Youthful confidence, I suppose, or perhaps it was simply that I felt I had no alternative, there was nothing else I could do.'

I had never heard him talk so much. I said, 'I suppose you're right, there never seems a clear-cut choice at the time. It's only later on, when you look back at something you've done, that you see it was really a milestone and you could have gone off in some quite different direction. When you get to – well – our age,' I said, perhaps to flatter him.

He had a way of stretching his long jaw forward when he was pleased. 'Maybe it's not the milestones that matter but the road in between. That's something you'll find out when you really *are* my age.'

Daddy is quite a philosopher, I could hear Mrs Hobbs saying. I felt as if I was at a milestone now, on the threshold of something. Waiting to step over.

I looked at Mr Hobbs. Still smiling with pleasure, he swung the car up round a steep bend. A deep valley of stone fell away beneath us; the glittering air danced above it.

I said, 'I left Richard once. About ten years ago. His mother got ill and I went back. I didn't make up my mind, it was made up for me. Or so it seemed at the time. Now I wonder – perhaps I wanted to go back, really, but didn't want to admit it. Too proud, or didn't want the responsibility. So I was glad to feel I had no choice, that I was forced . . .'

He gave his apologetic cough. 'I'm sure you did the right thing. And that's what matters after all. *What* you do, not why you do it.'

'But motives do matter, surely? If you do something for what are really irrelevant reasons, you do it badly. I mean, to keep a marriage together out of inertia or duty, if you don't, well, love . . .'

What was love? Lying on your back in a buttercup meadow?

'Don't you think there's too much talk nowadays about feelings and motives? I read a lot of modern novels, you know. It seems to me that people torture themselves unnecessarily. Duty is a much easier conception, really.'

I was annoyed by this old man, smiling.

'I don't want to dry up, to be unemotional – to see nothing but actions being right or wrong! I want to *feel* something.'

Some people of forty are dead already, fixed like waxworks; I didn't want to be like that.

'Why did you leave your husband?' Mr Hobbs said 'your husband' as if he didn't much like Richard, and for some reason this pleased me.

'I can hardly remember now.' The senses forget; you only remember in your mind, like a story. 'I think I thought we had nothing more to say to each other. We'd been married ten years, that's always supposed to be a bad time. I was thirty. I suppose I resented – oh, all the things women are supposed to resent. Being a domestic machine, being diminished – all fashionable nonsense, really.' I laughed, suddenly embarrassed. 'I'm afraid I took myself very seriously.'

'No one else will, if you don't. It's necessary to believe in your own importance.'

'Do you?'

'I'm an old man.' He glanced sideways at me. '*You* are more interesting.' He reddened slightly as if he thought this a bold remark.

The road led giddily downwards. At the far end of this valley, we could see pinkish earth walls, the green fingers of an oasis. We drove into the dusty town. Out of the car, the sun was like a heavy hand. We took wine, bread, and some cheese we had bought, processed stuff in a packet, and sat under a palm tree. I wondered if Mr Hobbs would quote from Omar Khayyám. The wine was warm as tea and the cheese had liquified: we poured it on to our barley bread. Children crowded round us; ants crawled in the dust.

The children watched us, big-eyed. Mr Hobbs gave them his bread and cheese. 'It's too hot to eat,' he said. The children pressed closer. 'We could do with some loaves and fishes,' Mr Hobbs said and looked embarrassed, as if it was shameful to care about other people's hunger. A little boy came up with lumps of rock in his hand. One was curved like a shell; in its depths, pale amethyst glinted. Mr Hobbs put his hand in his pocket.

He bought the rock and gave it to me. More children appeared, springing from nowhere. They mobbed us like birds; a bigger boy, lounging in the doorway of a house, came up and shouted at them, waving his arms in anger. He said, 'I am sorry for this annoyance. They have not good manners. I must tell you that the road from here is broken.'

'Can't we go on?' I asked. The heat was appalling and I wasn't sorry, but it is always hard to turn back.

'The mountain has fallen,' he said. He was a thin boy in a striped burnouse, brown and white. He had a delicate, intelligent face. 'The army is moving it, but today there is no road.'

'We would have had to stay the night at Zagora, anyway. It's taken longer than I thought to get as far as this. I've been worrying about that.' Mr Hobbs looked at me shyly. I wondered, with amusement, whether he had been afraid I might

mind, might feel he was – what was the old-fashioned word?
– *compromising* me.

'Perhaps it's just as well, then. Your wife would have worried.'

He nodded. 'I don't like to leave her at night. That's the worst time for her, she gets afraid when she wakes in the night.'

We thanked the boy, congratulated him on his English, walked back to the car. I wondered if we should have given him something for his information, but he seemed too dignified.

'How ill is she?'

'More than she knows.' He hesitated. 'We don't talk about it. It's important she should have hope.'

'I don't agree.' He put the remains of our picnic, one empty bottle, two glasses and the cheese wrappers, into a bag in the boot of the car. I was giddy with the heat and a little flown with the wine. 'I really don't agree. One should be able to face death,' I cried earnestly, standing in the middle of this desert town and shouting at the sun.

'You're still very young,' he said. It was a pompous remark but he spoke it hesitantly. He touched my hand and said, 'You'll get heat stroke. One doesn't realize how strong the sun is. I think you should get into the car.'

I thought he would say something else, but he didn't. Perhaps he couldn't bear to, perhaps it was just that he felt *his* marriage to be a private affair. This annoyed me, so when he said as we were driving off, 'What you were telling me – what happened ten years ago – did it work out all right?' I replied in a stiff ironic voice.

'Oh, it all worked out for the best.'

'Please don't be angry with me,' he said, with humble directness, and I was sorry at once. He paused a minute and went on, 'You know, my generation don't often discuss these things with other people. I find it refreshing.'

'I didn't mean to be angry. It really was all right. We're used to each other now, we're furniture in each other's lives.'

'That's just an attitude, isn't it? I mean, you're really quite happy together?' He spoke anxiously, as if he really cared about this, and I thought: what a nice man he is. 'Of course,' he said, 'I know that nowadays people conduct their marriages differently. They don't take so much notice of the things we used to, like fidelity and so on.'

His hands were trembling slightly on the wheel. *Dirty old man* was what Richard would say. It seemed somehow shamefully out of date to admit to faithfulness: we have this idea now that sex is socially constructive, that delinquency and dictatorship spring from abstinence. It may, of course, be right. I said, 'I suppose we can't believe, any longer, that the purely physical thing matters so much.'

'What does then? I ask in a spirit of humble inquiry.'

He laughed. He seemed to be enjoying a feeling that he was taking part in a daring conversation. He must have been a very attractive man once, I thought, and then wondered, suddenly, if Adam had had a similar thought about me.

'Not being lonely, I suppose. Holding each other up. You have to make your own terms.'

Not that I have, I thought. I have been passive, carried along like a twig in a torrent. Should I have cried halt? How could I, without a reason? Richard had never given me one. Must one always have a reason, an excuse, to show the world like a certificate of release?

'What do you think of marriage?'

He shrugged his shoulders.

'Children?'

'I used to think, sometimes, that I'd built a house for strangers to live in. That I was just a father, a husband – I'd somehow ceased to exist as a person in my own right.' He smiled. 'Though now I'm contented enough and fond of my granddaughters.'

'That sounds sad.'

'Does it? I suppose everyone had the feeling sometime or other that they'd like to be free, walk out, wander over the earth. Most men, anyway.'

'*I* feel like that,' I said indignantly. 'Men and women aren't so different!'

'Vive la différence,' he said, and grinned so cheerfully at this silly joke that I couldn't help smiling back. Why shouldn't he be cheerful and silly? He had lugged his poor wife round for so long, like a heavy suitcase. Away from her, he must feel like a boy let out of school. Poor old man, I thought, and when he said, with his 'daring' look, 'This is a great treat for me, you know. I don't often get the chance to take out such an attractive young woman,' and put his hand on my knee, I put my hand on top of his and held it there.

'There's an anecdote in a Shaw play. *The Doctor's Dilemma*, I think. A young man asked his grandmother when he would be free from the temptations of love, and she said she didn't know.' He squeezed my hand and looked at me. 'You aren't happy, are you? I wish I could make you happy,' he said, so sweetly and gently that I was ashamed of the laughter building up inside me, and of the thought, *why he's old enough to be my father*. My father was not very old, of course. If he was still alive, he would be about Mr Hobbs's age. 'How old are you?' I wanted to ask, but he would be hurt by that, not understanding. I had never thought about my father, about meeting him, not knowing, and something like this happening, and now I saw it was possible, the desire to laugh became a fearful compulsion.

I pulled my mouth stiff. I heard my voice shaking. I've been very happy today. I've enjoyed being with you.'

'It's sweet of you to say that. But then you *are* sweet. Sweet and beautiful and good.' His voice had gone husky, his fingers were interlaced with mine. We were coming up to a twist in the precipitous road; as we swung round it, the wheels screamed and we seemed to swerve towards the edge of the precipice. Below me, the earth fell away; I saw cruel, dark rocks, ridged like basalt. I am afraid of heights. 'For God's sake,' I shouted, 'keep your hands on the *wheel*!'

He snatched his hand away. We were round the bend now

and my panic ebbed. 'I'm sorry,' I said. 'I was just awfully scared suddenly.'

He said nothing for a minute. Then, very stiffly, 'I am afraid I offended you.'

'Goodness me, no.' I laughed. 'What an old-fashioned word, anyway.'

'I'm an old man,' he said. 'I use old-fashioned words.'

I couldn't bear the mournful look on his face. 'You're not so old. Certainly, I don't think of you as being old.' The sad look remained, blackmailing me. 'In fact,' I said loudly, 'if you really want to know, I think of you as a very attractive man.'

Elizabeth is such a nice woman, she cannot bear to hurt anyone.

Chapter Fifteen

Mrs Hobbs was on the terrace of the hotel, lying in a long chair with her legs up. A fat woman, resting on the beach at Bournemouth. She fanned herself with a magazine.

'What a nice surprise. We didn't expect you back yet.'

'We only got halfway. The road was blocked after that, a landslide or something. Has Richard been looking after you?'

'They took me to see the dancing. It was interesting but a bit comical, really. Not so much dancing, you know, but a lot of waggling about and a queer kind of singing. We all had lunch together and a nice talk. They went up to rest afterwards.'

I went up to our room. I opened the door gently, in case Richard was asleep.

Flora was lying on the bed, the sheet across her legs. Arms crossed behind her head, white breasts pointing upwards. Water was running; from the shower, Richard called out something that I couldn't catch, and Flora laughed, her head turned away from me, her small breasts bouncing. I shut the door and walked down the corridor. My legs felt as if they had gone to sleep: I trod painfully on nothing. I went down the stairs and out to the terrace. 'Richard's fast asleep,' I said. 'I thought I wouldn't wake him.'

'Have a nice cup of tea,' Mrs Hobbs suggested. 'Though they make it in bags here, elephant tea they call it, isn't that funny?'

I twisted my face into an exaggerated smile like a woman at a cocktail party. I sat down beside Mrs Hobbs and faced the view from the terrace. There was a cypress with bougainvillea climbing up it, and beyond, a landscape of red hills. Trees and red hills and flies buzzing.

'Order her some tea, Daddy,' Mrs Hobbs said.

He was looking at me in a puzzled way. 'Do you want tea?'

'I'd love some.'

I was blushing. My whole body was one, burning blush. I had been safe, hiding in a house like someone in a tomb, only alive in dreams. This had happened before, in a dream. Was it any different?

Their faces were anxious. 'Perhaps it would be better if you had a nice lie down,' Mrs Hobbs was saying. 'You look a bit queer. Doesn't she look a bit queer, Daddy?'

'I feel perfectly all right,' I said.

My head was full of sound, a high, piercing note that seemed to ring from the desert and reach the terrace in waves.

'She's going off,' Mrs Hobbs said.

I closed my eyes, fighting against the cold waves of faintness; they enclosed me in ice and receded, leaving me numb, facing the red horizon.

Mr Hobbs's hand was under my arm. 'I'll take you upstairs to your room,' he said, raising me up as if I weighed nothing. I felt weightless, light as a ballet dancer. Mr Hobbs's lean, worried face bobbed against my vision. His hand was under my elbow.

'Come along now,' he said masterfully.

He propelled me off the terrace and through the shuttered dining-room. There were wicker chairs in the dark bar; in one of them a soldier stretched out, snoring. 'Let me sit down a minute,' I begged.

'Better to go straight upstairs. You need to lie down. I'll take you up to your room.'

'I'd rather stay here. I'm so tired. Please.'

'Bed's the best place, then.' He put his arms round my waist. 'I'll come with you, you'll be all right. Only a little effort, then you can lie down and be comfortable.'

In spite of his slender appearance, he was very strong. His arm was a tight bar of muscle. Appalled, I fought against him, pressing myself back, making my body leaden. He gripped one hand on the banister.

I pleaded. 'I don't want to go up. There's no need. I'm all right now, really.'

I relaxed against him. I could have leaned my head on his breast and cried.

'Sure?' He lowered me into a chair at the foot of the stairs and stood above me critically. 'You don't look it. It was too much for you, all that heat. I should have taken better care of you.' He smiled and stretched his jaw. 'I feel responsible, you know. But if you'd really rather stay here, I'll go and fetch your husband. Your room's number nineteen, isn't it?'

'*No*.' It was an explosive, ludicrous sound in the cool dark. The soldier woke up with a snort; his head jerked up and he looked at us inquiringly. I made myself smile. It was like ripping off plaster. 'Richard hasn't been well,' I said, 'I'd rather let him sleep. He's had this nasty go of dysentery, it's left him really rather weak.'

Mr Hobbs's expression was gently distasteful. 'I'm sorry, but I think I should fetch him. You think too much of others, Elizabeth, you should think of yourself more.'

I was filled with horror and shame at my failure to antici-pate this situation. Because I *had* known of it. I had only pre-tended I didn't know, preferring to see things as I would like them to be, rather than as they were, imprisoning myself in a ramshackle edifice of lies because I couldn't bear to knock it down and start again, shivering and alone in a great expanse of sand. And now a shabby mischance had destroyed it, knocked down the precarious walls of my prison, I still sat on in the wreckage and kept my eyes closed, safe behind broken bars.

I laughed. 'You know, you're wrong there. I think of myself all the time. And I'm really being enormously selfish at this moment, because what I want is not Richard fussing around – and he *does* fuss, you know – but just to go back to the terrace and have tea. So if you really want to be kind, that's what you'll let me do.'

'Well – just for a little while, then,' he said, relenting – and perhaps enjoying the fact that he had something to relent about, was in command of the situation.

We walked back to the terrace. He kept his hand on my arm. I thought: this isn't happening, it's a dream. And then: oh, *please*, if there have to be more lies, at least let me only tell them to other people, not to myself any more.

I smiled at Mrs Hobbs. I said brazenly, 'I've come back for tea, after all.'

I lay in a chair, weak and convalescent, while Mr Hobbs poured tea and waited on us both. He talked about the day, the road, the heat, the liquified cheese, the children at the oasis. He was a born nurse, settling his patients comfortably, diverting their minds with bland conversation. Was this a habit he had grown into over the years or had he always been like this, turning his wife into an invalid before there was any real need, a man who could only see himself in a solicitous relationship with other people? I would never know. He was fixed for me in this time, this pose.

I said, 'I feel so stupid, making such a fuss.'

They beamed on me fondly. I felt luxuriously comfortable with them, a child safe in a parent's lap. Mrs Hobbs said, 'This heat is dangerous when you aren't used to it. I know I shall be glad to get back across the Atlas. We're going tomorrow, aren't we, Daddy?'

Mr Hobbs nodded. He spoke, rather flatly, of an early start before the heat really got going, and promised his wife air-conditioned comfort in the hotel at Marrakesh.

'I wish I was coming,' I said. We were to stay a few days longer here, for Flora's sake. She had introductions to various families in this district from a professor at the London School of Economics. I felt the present hit me like a blow in the back. I had thought of the Hobbses as shielding me like parents, but the nursery comfort was illusory.

'Why don't you, then?'

I explained about Flora's book and the professor's introductions.

'But surely, if *you* find the heat trying, your husband wouldn't want to stay. . . .' Mrs Hobbs looked amazed: a wife's comfort is always the first consideration. 'After all, Mrs Dove was expecting to make her own way, wasn't she? I'm sure she wouldn't want to put you out, when you're feeling so ill.'

Mr Hobbs smiled at her. 'My dear, you mustn't interfere with other people's arrangements.'

A look passed between husband and wife.

'I was only thinking of Elizabeth,' she said, with some indignation.

When they went upstairs at last, I stayed on the terrace. 'I'm so lazy,' I said, laughing gaily.

I lay in the chair, waiting. People came on to the terrace. I dared not turn my head. My muscles began to ache. Someone had left an English Sunday newspaper behind on the table. I read it through twice: a general's serialized memoirs; a critical article which expressed disappointment with new books from two leading novelists. It grew a little cooler. I felt sodden with sleepiness. The sunset opened like an orange flower above the desert. The cypresses in the garden turned black.

Richard came on to the terrace. He was wearing a blue shirt, a crimson scarf knotted round his neck. 'So you're *back*. Why didn't you come up? I was worried about you.'

'I was coming to find you in a minute. But we've only just got back.'

'You look a bit gone.'

'I feel it, I assure you.'

'Why are you talking like someone in a novel?'

'Am I? People in novels must sound like people in real life sometimes.'

'Never. All those ums and ahs.'

He sat beside me. He looked terribly well.

I said, 'You look terribly well. Did you enjoy your day?'

He frowned at the sunset as if blaming it for something. 'Moderately.' He smiled. 'I missed you.'

'Oh.'

'You should say, "I'm glad".'

'I'm glad.'

He hummed under his breath for a minute. When he stopped, the silence expanded and filled the sky.

I said, 'Why don't you talk to me?'

He looked surprised. 'I am talking to you.' He looked round for inspiration. 'It's a lovely sunset.'

'Gorgeous.'

He sighed. 'That's a silly word.'

'Why?'

'Don't know.' He made an effort. 'Vamps in the 'twenties were gorgeous. Courtesans in the eighteenth century.'

'You mean only loose women are gorgeous?'

'Loose women? Heavens, no. Ecclesiastical garments, too. Purple and gold raiment.'

'But not sunsets?' I saw Flora coming on to the terrace. I laughed and thrashed my hand up and down on the arm of my chair in an ecstasy of amusement. 'Oh, my dear Richard, you are silly.'

'Joke?' said Flora, pausing a little way away. She looked cool and rested in a white dress with a chaste gold chain round her throat. I wished words like 'chaste' and 'loose' would refrain from slipping into my mind: I was terrified of giving myself away.

'Not really.' Richard got up and balanced on the ball of one foot as if he had been seized by an attack of cramp.

'I'm just hysterical with exhaustion,' I said, smiling up at Flora until my face felt as if it would crack. As if *I* would crack. 'I've had such a marvellous day, I can't tell you,' I cried. I laughed like a brass gong.

Richard's puzzled look alarmed me. I have just got back, I told myself. Remember that. I feel rather guilty because Richard has been worried about me.

I thought: if Mr Hobbs tells him we came back early, Richard will know. We know so much about each other.

'Tell us about it,' Flora said. She sat gracefully down on a low chair. She was small and neat and clean; beside her I felt enormous, a great, dusty peasant with huge thighs. 'Richard,' Flora said, putting her head charmingly on one side, 'I'm sure poor Liz could do with a drink. *I* could, I know.'

No one calls me Liz. *No one.* How dare she! I felt myself inflating slowly with rage, like a tyre. Does she think, because she has slept with my husband, she can call me Liz?

'I must go and change first.' I heaved myself out of my chair with elaborate sighs. 'I really am filthy.' My huge legs ached. I toppled towards them and smiled.

'We'll have a drink waiting for you,' Flora said, and put her dark glasses on. In dark glasses, white dress, gold chain, she sat and looked at the sky. 'What a heavenly sunset.'

'Isn't "heavenly" rather an emotive word?' I said.

I walked through the dining-room, smiling, my head on one side, humming between clenched teeth. In the bar, I saw Mr Hobbs looking at me: I wondered if he thought me deranged. I went up to him and said, 'Please don't tell Richard we got back so early. Apparently he was a bit worried, so I said – oh, it sounds silly – that we'd only just got back, that I'd just sat down. . . .'

'Of course.' He looked much younger in the dark bar; his gentle, chivalrous face smiling.

124

'And you see, if you tell him I hadn't felt well, he'd be so cross with me for not waking him up.' I spoke in a childish voice, like a little girl begging for sweets.

'I told you he'd feel like that, didn't I? Don't worry. I won't say a word.'

'Will you explain to your wife?'

'She'll understand. She knows what husbands are.'

We smiled at each other like conspirators. I felt I had handled the situation marvellously.

You handled him all right, didn't you? I said aloud, in the bedroom. I looked in the mirror and pulled my mouth into strange shapes, apeing bewilderment, comic dismay, tragic dignity. Everything seemed to have moved on to a level of fantasy. 'You've got dinner to get through, dearie,' I said, grinning at my reflection like a cheerful char in a pantomime. 'The play's the thing.'

I stripped off my clothes and dropped them in heaps on the floor. I stood under the shower. There was a heavy sensation in my stomach: apart from this feeling, which was too dull for pain, my body was uninhabited. I – or something – moved this empty body about, drying it, covering it with clean clothes, brushing its hair, painting colour and expression on to its round blob of face, tenderly examining a new wrinkle under its left eye. I took a hand mirror and examined this wrinkle from the side, frowning to deepen it. There was a tap at the door and I slid the mirror guiltily into the pocket of my dress.

'Come in.'

Flora opened the door. 'Are you all right? I was coming up to get something, so I thought I'd see. . . . We thought you looked a bit out of sorts.'

Coming up to get what? An ear-ring, left behind in the bed? Did she forget her pants? I watched to see where her eyes wandered. Everyone has doubts, surely, in this situation? But she was looking at me with simple, concerned inquiry. I thought: did I dream it, then?

Perhaps they had been discussing me. Richard had said,

'I wonder if she's guessed. Though she said nothing to me. Perhaps you should go up and have a word with her, make sure . . . !'

That would be typical of Richard. He likes to get other people – usually me, of course – to do the dirty work: make the awkward telephone call, tell the gardener who comes for four hours a week that he has ruined the asparagus bed, speak to Tom's teacher about his appalling arithmetic.

Poor Flora. I said. 'No, I'm fine. Really. Just a bit tired.'

'Oh. Good. Will you be down soon? Richard's fretting about dinner.'

She smiled, but seemed faintly surprised by this. You'll learn, my girl, I thought.

'I'll be down soon.'

'Shall I wait for you?'

'No. I won't be long. Keep the brute company. Or go on in, I don't mind. I'm not hungry, I'll miss out the first course anyway.'

'All right.'

She hesitated a minute, or perhaps I only thought she did. Then she smiled, waved her hand weakly, and was gone. I put a suitcase on the bed and began to throw clothes into it, half my dresses so that Richard wouldn't notice when he hung his trousers up in the wardrobe, but all my underwear, since he would not look in my drawer. When the case was almost full, my hands were trembling, though I felt decisive and cool. Or saw myself as feeling decisive and cool. I closed the lid, snapping the locks, and stood the case against the wall. I put another case in front of it, an empty one, and suddenly thought of an old story in a childhood book. Cromwell's men were searching a Cavalier household; the man had hidden in a window-seat and on top of it his wife had placed their sleeping child. There was a coloured picture of the little boy: ringlets and a lace collar. I thought: that story is relevant to nothing, but I shall remember it until my dying day. Perhaps, by then, I shall have forgotten this. What is important?

I went down to dinner.

Chapter Sixteen

We all drank too much. Richard kept filling glasses. He was solicitous, like Mr Hobbs. Like a waiter. Flora laughed a lot. She had a gold filling in one of her back teeth. I remember her, head thrown back in the middle of some joke she was making, and that sudden glint of gold, like treasure in a cave.

After dinner, nothing seemed worth bothering about. We went to bed. I was too tired to clean my teeth. Richard moved about in the bathroom; the light hurt my eyes so I turned on my stomach and hid my face in the pillow.

When I woke, it was dark. I was sweating and giddy. I sat on the edge of the bed and felt the earth rolling. I got up and walked to the window. The blue night was full of stars; somewhere a dog barked rhythmically. There was a hollow core of sadness inside me, a sad, empty hole.

Richard said, 'What's up? Can't you sleep?'

'How long has it been going on?'

'What?'

'How long has it been going on?'

'I don't know what you're talking about.' The words drawled out sleepily but there was enough light from the window now to see that his eyes were open, watching me. I felt as if I were suffocating. I must be crazy, I thought, and tried to breathe deeply and steadily.

'Do you feel ill?' he asked hopefully.

'I wish I did.' It would be better than feeling nothing. And if I were ill, someone else would take over, I need not go on with this. I saw myself subsiding comfortably to the cool floor, my mouth full of moans. *Elizabeth is not well enough to discuss anything, she needs rest and peace.* If I held my breath long enough, I could make myself faint. It was a trick I had learned at school, to get out of netball. I remained still and upright, facing into the room, an accusing figure in a nightdress.

Richard gave a long, whistling sigh. 'All right. How did you know?'

'I came up. We got back about four o'clock. I lied about that.'

'Oh. Oh. I see.' A sly embarrassment came into his voice. 'Were we ... I mean ...'

'You were in the bathroom at the time.'

'Oh.'

There was a long pause during which a kind of stage fright seized me and perhaps him too: we remained in our positions, Richard sitting up in bed and me standing at the window, looking at each other helplessly like actors who have forgotten their lines.

Richard said in a low voice, 'I'm sorry.' Silence. He groaned. 'Oh God, what can I say? I don't know if it makes any difference, but it wasn't planned. It was just something that happened. I suppose we had too much to drink at lunch. This local wine is deceptive.' His tone became more confident, slightly indignant. 'We only had a bottle.'

'Very abstemious of you.'

He sighed again, like wind in a tunnel. 'I didn't expect you'd be back much before seven.'

'I hadn't imagined you'd laid on the show for my benefit.'

'All right. *All right*.' He shot out of bed and poured out a glass of mineral water. Holding it against his chest, he stood in the middle of the room. 'Look, it meant nothing. We had this wine at lunch and we came up to snooze ...'

'Together?'

He didn't answer.

I said, 'For God's sake, you don't have to be a *gentleman*. I mean, the sensible thing would have been to go to her room, wouldn't it? In case I came back.'

He said reluctantly, 'She came here. I was half asleep. She wanted an aspirin.'

'Oh.'

'She had a headache.'

'I'm sorry. I hope it got better.'

'*Shut up.*'

'I really don't see why I should.'

'No. There's no reason why you should.'

'Well, then.' I began to feel sick. I said, 'Don't you see, there are some things I have to know?'

'Ask them. Go on.' He sat down on the edge of the bed and drank the mineral water, very slowly. 'God, I feel ill,' he muttered, and rasped his hand over his chin.

'I'm sorry.' I did feel sorry. He had had dysentery. He was on holiday. He needed this trip: he was a conscientious man who drove himself hard. He had been looking forward to 'getting away' as he put it, perhaps because it sounded more therapeutic than 'going on holiday'.

'It doesn't matter. How I feel doesn't matter. I mean that. I didn't mean to blackmail you.' He smiled up at me.

'Well.' I wanted to ask, did he love her, but the word embarrassed me. 'Was this the first time?'

'Yes.'

'I don't mean on this trip. Other times. Before.'

He said nothing.

'Please tell me. I'll try not to be angry.'

'I don't care if you are. Oh – I don't mean it like that. What I mean is, what I mind about is if you *mind*.'

'I can't not mind, just to make you feel comfortable.'

'No. Do you mind, though?'

'Yes.'

'Why?'

'*Why?*'

'Why?' He was glaring at me suddenly. 'After all, you don't want me, do you, you haven't for years.'

'That's not my fault.'

'I didn't say it was. But it's a fact, though. Isn't it?'

'Perhaps it makes it worse. I feel guilty.'

'I'm bored to tears with your feeling guilty. For Christ's sake, it's not a virtuous *substitute*. Or do you think it is?'

'I don't know. No, of course it's not. I'm sorry.'

'Jesus wept.'

'How long has it been going on? I asked in the beginning. You didn't tell me.'

'Do you want a tally? How many times?'

'No. Oh, *please*. I just want to know. The time we lived in London?'

'No.'

'Please tell me the truth. I can't bear anything else now.'

'I've given you one answer. If you don't like it, you can have the other.'

'Before Oliver was born?'

'Perhaps. I can't remember your exact gynaecological state.'

'Where?'

'Oh, Christ. The back of the car. Parks and open spaces. At her flat. Anything else?'

'How long did it go on for?'

'Eighteen months. Two years. I wasn't the only one, you know. The thing you should understand, it doesn't mean much to Flora.'

'You mean she takes her sex like a man?'

'If you like. She's not nympho or anything. It's just – well – like continuing the conversation.'

I said, 'In masculine-dominated societies, the only women who have a chance of rational conversation with men are the tarts.'

'She's not a tart.'

'You mean you never paid her?'

'Try not to be a bitch.'

'Well, you must have bought her dinner, drinks and so forth. At that time, we were rather badly off.'

'Flora always paid for her own drinks.'

'Round for round, like a man?'

He said slowly and dangerously, 'I daresay I might have been four bob down at the end of an evening. You could say it was cheaper than taking you out. In that case, I would have paid for *all* the drinks, wouldn't I? But you wouldn't come out with me, would you?'

'You always wanted me to go to parties. You knew I hated parties.'

'It didn't matter that I was bored without you?'

'Dear God. You were *grown-up*. Did you ever think of me?'

'Most of the time.'

'Did you talk me over with Flora?'

'Perhaps once or twice. I was *unhappy*. She said – perhaps this will amuse you – that the trouble was I was really a rather feminine man and I needed a masculine woman to complement me.'

'I am a feminine woman?'

'That was the line.'

'What a load of crap.'

'Maybe. We were younger then.'

'Afterwards. After the eighteen months were up, what happened?'

'She got married again, I suppose.'

'You suppose?'

'She married Dove.'

'How did you feel about that?'

'Relieved, chiefly. I hoped she'd be happy. She'd not had a particularly happy life, you know.'

'Did it go on?'

He looked at me. It was growing lighter in the room. His face was stubbly and tired.

I spelled it out. 'Have you made love to her since? Since that time before she married Dove? Between then and now.'

'Intermittently.'

'What does that mean?'

He said with irritation, 'Just what I say. We met from time to time. Every now and again, not often. Sometimes we did, sometimes we didn't.' The blood came up into his face and he shouted, 'Oh – stop looking like a bloody martyr. You didn't suffer. And there was no reason *not* to. It wasn't like taking up with someone new, no point in making a *stand*.'

'She might have laughed at you?'

'God, you do hate me, don't you?'

'No.'

'Of course you do. You've got a right to.'

'No one has any right to hate anyone.'

'Right – wrong. . . . Oh, you fool, you damned, righteous *fool*. D'you know what you are? You're a married *virgin*. What's so marvellous about you that you have to keep it safe, keep yourself *intact*?'

'I hate you,' I said. 'I hate you. I loathe you, you make me sick, *sick*. . . .' I hurled myself at him; he rolled over on his back and drew up his knees to protect himself. 'I wish you were dead,' I shouted, grabbing hold of his hair.

Someone began thumping on the wall. We froze in this foolish posture. An outraged voice spoke several loud, guttural words.

'What did he say?'

'I don't know.' We were both whispering. Richard sat up. 'It's the German. You know, the one in shorts. He sat at the next table at dinner.'

'Oh God. *Richard*.'

'What?'

'How awful.' My heart felt like a stone. I thought: how shall I face Flora? I said, 'I mean, we'll have to face him in the morning.'

'Oh, grow *up*.' Richard spoke in a savage undertone. 'It doesn't matter. For God's sake, you're nearly forty. You still act like a bloody adolescent.'

'That's fine. That's just fine, from you.' I was crouched on the bed like a woman in a Thurber drawing. 'Stop bullying me, will you? You're a frightful bully, I feel sometimes as if I'm being hammered *flat*. Do you know what Willy said? He said, "Has Richard stopped bullying you yet?" '

'Who's Willy?' he asked, amazed.

'Oh – it doesn't matter. Oh – I feel so awful.' I stretched out on the bed, moaning.

He put his arms round me. 'Oh, my darling, my honey bee. I'm sorry. It's all my fault. I'm sorry.'

He began to cry. It seemed like strategy. I felt cold as marble.

'I'm going out for a walk,' I said.

He fumbled in his pyjama pocket for a handkerchief. He blew his nose. 'Do you want me to come?'

'No.'

He touched my hand. 'This sort of thing happens. It's not just what I've done. We're in the middle of our lives, what do we want to do with the rest of them? It all happens so quickly, it's hard to make sense of it. But we have to try. Do you know what I'm talking about?'

'I think so.' I wanted to weep but I felt nothing, only a generalized sadness. All this pain and weakness cramped in the small trap of my skull; one sharp blow would end it. Death ends everything, so why should we bother?

'You look worn out,' I said. 'Try and go to sleep.'

Outside the hotel, the road led upwards to the top of the fort. The stars had faded and a broad band of pinkish light spread over the desert; the dogs had stopped barking at last. A few huddled figures rested against the parapet. They didn't move as I walked along and there was no sound except the crunch of my feet on the gritty road. When I stopped, there was silence; silence and emptiness without and within. Everything had stopped.

I leaned against the parapet. The air was so dry that my cheeks burned with it. The early morning was still and beautiful; I felt too tired, too heavy and puffy for this beautiful world. I should have loved Richard. There was no other way of containing sadness, of healing over that open, weeping sore. Action couldn't heal it, only love or death, and death was easier. I thought: this is why men go to war.

There was a knot inside me that had tightened over the years, not loosened. There were many ways to explain this; we know so much about people now, taking their minds apart like clocks, but it mends nothing. My mind was frigid like my body, cold and ungenerous. You're worth nothing, I thought, why don't you *die*.

An engine stuttered in the pure air. Looking down, I could see the hotel steps, dusted pink with fine sand, and the Hobbs's car. The porter was carrying out the luggage. Mrs Hobbs came down the steps, wearing a navy blue two-piece and carrying a white straw handbag. She wore a white linen hat, the kind women wear to play bowls in suburban parks. She walked towards her car treading solemnly, the way heavy people do, as if each step was a religious occasion.

Mr Hobbs looked up towards the parapet. I caught my breath. I couldn't die, I couldn't love, but I could run. I struck a bargain with God. If he waves, I thought, I shall know what to do. Mr. Hobbs was looking towards me. Decision hung by a hair.

He lifted his arm and I ran down, smiling.

Chapter Seventeen

'I'm glad you decided to stay with Richard,' Aunt Lilian said.

That episode was over and forgotten now, stuck in the family album like the picture of Tom as captain of the cricket team in his last year at primary school. But Aunt Lilian was dying; time had telescoped for her.

'Anything else would have been rather impractical, wouldn't it?'

I kept my voice low and smiled, a bright, cheerful smile for the sickroom.

She gave a little sigh. I thought she was tired. It wasn't until afterwards that I wondered if this answer had disappointed her. Had she hoped I would say I loved him?

'Practical,' she said, with scorn.

She closed her eyes. The lids were white and papery, like butterfly wings. What remained of her hair was ragged and cottony as tags of sheep wool caught in the hedgerows. With her eyes closed, she looked already dead. She had no one, no husband, no lover, no child, only me. I took her light, dry hand and held it.

'*Practical*,' she repeated.

'Dear Aunt Lilian,' I said, 'it does come into it. Divorce is a messy business.'

Two of our friends had recently been divorced: one had embarked on a second marriage. In these troubles, Richard and I played our vicarious parts: we were an old, safely married couple, our centrally heated house with books, whisky, grubby paw-marks on the walls, was a refuge for the battle-scarred. We listened to tales of betrayal and high-principled resolve, offered cigarettes and wise advice, and, when the sessions were over, passed judgement in private. It seemed to us – the weary recipients of all this self-torture, this heavy tossing aside of responsibilities – ridiculous that anyone should go to such tortuous and sincerely unhappy lengths to terminate one unsatisfactory relationship only to replace it by another that might well be equally unsatisfactory, perhaps even more so because the odds stacked against it would be heavier. Faults that might have been endured in a first marriage would become intolerable in a second: an infidelity, for example, a mere slip before divorce, would be unbearable afterwards, a direct attack on a shakier, less well-defended stronghold. Nor could you complain, without ridicule, of *two* bad-tempered husbands we told ourselves, wagging our wise heads and laughing. And for a second failure there would be no possibility of comfort, no recourse to friends – besieged once – or to parents, hurt enough already.

Children, of course, presented an even greater difficulty. The business of custody and access was always arranged with the maximum of inconvenience to all parties. Richard's father who had been a 'gentleman' and allowed his wife to divorce him, could not bear to see her, nor go to the flat where she had taken Richard immediately the proceedings were over, to live with 'Uncle John'. Nor could Nonni bear to see *him* – though Richard insisted this was empty protest on her part, in case she should be thought lacking in sensitivity. She used to take Richard, then four, to the park and leave him standing by the boating pond while she hid out of sight behind the shelter. The time he had to wait alone was terrible. He used to jump up and down and sing at the top of his voice to comfort himself and when his father came along he always said the same thing, 'Well, you *are* a merry little grig!' They always walked round the park, ending up at the café by the bandstand where his father drank tea and Richard ate an ice. Then they would go back to the pond and his father would take a newspaper out of his pocket and make a paper boat.

'They were marvellous boats,' Richard told me. 'He had a talent for that sort of thing – though not for much else, I believe. They were *boats*, not just cocked hats, sailing. I used to love to watch him, he was so quick and you could never quite see how he did it, it was like a conjurer. But I suppose I got bored, or just older – I know that in the end I was longing for a wooden boat with a proper sail but I couldn't ask and he never realized. It wasn't his fault, if you only see a child once a month, you can't be expected to know these things. But I remember that in the end I began to hate those damn paper boats, and I hated the smell of the pond. Stagnant water and dog dirt! There were always lots of old ladies with their pets; they used to come up and speak to me when I was waiting on my own and their beastly little brutes would sniff at my legs. I wasn't really frightened – I don't think so, anyway – but I used to scream and scream and they would fuss and say "Poor little boy, where's your naughty Mummy?" And she would dodge out from behind the shelter and watch for my father coming and dodge back – I suppose the whole business just became too difficult and embarrassing. He went to Australia when I was seven, but we must have stopped going to the park some time before that, because I can remember he used to send me postcards instead, comic ones, fat ladies and so on, and after he left the country he never wrote again. She'd got married again at this point, perhaps he thought a clean break was better. But I missed the cards. I remember I went on hoping for one for a long time. . . .'

Richard talked a lot about his childhood at this time. Perhaps he wasn't certain of me and wanted to appeal to my better nature. Or perhaps he needed to convince himself. I know I was convinced.

'What would we have done with Tom and Oliver?' I said to Aunt Lilian on her deathbed.

She opened her eyes.

'Kit,' she said. 'What will happen to Kit?'

'Don't worry about her, darling. I'll look after her.'

'I shouldn't die,' Aunt Lilian said.

She never spoke again. She became unconscious. There were red patches on her cheeks and she breathed in little snores. She wet the bed. The district nurse who lived next door helped me, rolling her to one side while I pulled out the draw sheet. Her white legs had gone little, like a child's; the crinkly grey hair on her pubis seemed an absurdity. She weighed nothing. The nurse said, 'You know you'd think you'd get used to it, but you never do. Let's leave her the next time, don't disturb the poor soul.'

When she slipped into death, the nurse held a mirror to her lips and wept. She had been a pupil at Aunt Lilian's school. 'She was a wonderful woman,' she said, 'she was strict but just, you always knew where you were with her.'

Her's were the only tears, the only epitaph. Aunt Kit told me 'Lil' had gone on holiday to Rome and was indignant because she had been left behind. 'Your Aunt Lilian knew it was my life's ambition to go to Rome.'

Whether this was true, whether this resentment had any basis in their joint history, I never knew. Aunt Kit never mentioned it again and rarely mentioned her sister. Once or twice in the next years she would look at me in a puzzled way and say, 'When's Lil's train due in?' or 'She's been a long time, just doing a bit of shopping, hasn't she?' but that was all.

I took Aunt Kit home with me. The house was big enough – if anywhere was big enough to house Aunt Kit and Nonni. They had the two front rooms on the ground floor and at night we locked Aunt Kit in, so she shouldn't wander.

She was very little trouble, happy with a bottle of cooking sherry and a packet of cigarettes, playing the piano when she was sober and talking to the boys about Pitt the younger, which had been her special subject at school and on which her mind was perfectly clear, though it seemed, sometimes, that she believed him to be still alive. Tom and Oliver were fond of her, treating her like a younger child: at that time they both had a strong maternal streak. She would have been no trouble at all if it had not been for Nonni's fear that she would 'burn us all alive in our beds with her filthy smoking habits'. Nonni disliked her, fearing, I suppose, her innocent senility, and would hobble across the hall for the pleasure of looking into her room and complaining. 'Filthy, filthy, not fit for pigs,' though in fact the room was not dirty, only littered with old newspapers like Hampstead Heath on a bank holiday.

She said to Richard – what she did not dare say to me – that it would be sensible to try to get Aunt Kit into a home. 'Elizabeth is wearing herself out,' was the line they both took. And though I think Richard was, to some extent, genuinely worried on my account, his attitude was really the same as his mother's. Though he would never admit it, the sight of Aunt Kit in her old, man's dressing-gown, offended him. He hated our friends to see her. 'It isn't as if it would matter to her after all,' he argued. 'She doesn't know where she is, most of the time, nor who we are. And she's very strong, she may last for years. You can't go on indefinitely – after all, the time may come when you'll have to wash and dress her, look after her like a baby. . . .'

That time had already come, though I had concealed it from

Richard, bathing Aunt Kit every afternoon while Nonni was having her rest, and plaiting her long hair into two pigtails tied with ribbon.

'Someone has to look after her. Why shouldn't it be me? At least I love her and remember what she was like. I know some old people's homes are marvellously well run, but some aren't and you can't always tell. There are so many old people.'

'I know that. You're being marvellous, I know that too. But – for God's sake, Elizabeth – she may live to be a *hundred*. We'll be *sixty-five*.'

He looked suddenly frantic, as if he saw his old age galloping towards him like an express train. There were so many things he had planned to do: he had always been a man for plans and theories. We were to hire a boat and sail with the boys round the Mediterranean. We were to buy a house in Anatolia; there were places there where you could live for ten shillings a day and hunt wild boar. It meant more to him than a boat and a house in Turkey. He wanted to stretch out, touch something before he died. He glared at me as if I were a stranger who did not understand this. 'Don't *you* want to do something with your life?'

I was frozen with anger. 'I promised Aunt Lilian.'

'What are you atoning for?' Richard said.

Chapter Eighteen

At the top of the pass, Mr Hobbs stopped the car and walked back along the road a little way. 'I fear Nature calls,' he had explained. He was faintly embarrassed by this necessity: as if to compensate for it, he walked out of sight with a brisk, youthful step.

Mrs Hobbs and I sat on the stone which marked the top of the pass. The car was parked some way below with its doors open: a beetle with spread wings. Above us, the shadowed mountains, purple and veridian, lifted into the pure sky.

Mrs Hobbs had taken off her hat and replaced it with a white chiffon scarf. Stretched tautly over a metallic arrangement of hair grips, it looked like a mosquito net. She looked at me shyly and took my hand. 'You know, dear, I don't want to intrude . . .'

I had told them only that I couldn't bear another day in the heat and that Richard had thought it a good idea for me to go on if they were willing to take me. I had had no difficulty in leaving. When I went up to the room, Richard was sprawled out in an exhausted sleep, his mouth open. I scribbled a note and escaped. If the Hobbs had felt surprise at the speed with which I had packed my suitcase, they had not shown it. They seemed merely pleased to have my company and had not questioned the reason for it. Until now.

'Sometimes it helps to talk to someone,' Mrs Hobbs said.

'I know. But there's nothing wrong.'

At this moment, I believed this. I loved Richard. Now he was no longer here, expecting me to prove love to him, I could admit it. Perhaps this was too simple. Perhaps it was only that he had handed me my freedom and I could love him for that. I felt peaceful, sitting on this stone at the top of the pass; I was flooded with peace and happiness as with the sweet, cold air.

'I'm a meddlesome old woman.' She looked at me with comfortably accepted guilt, and I smiled at her, pressing her soft little hand. 'You can't help noticing things though, can you? Particularly if you're fond of someone. And we've got quite fond of you, you know, it's not just nosyness.'

Shut up, I begged her silently. Any minute now she would say something like *running away doesn't solve anything dear*, and I didn't want to hear her say that because I felt as if it *had* solved it. As if I had gone through some tunnel of experience and come out the other end stronger and more whole than

140

I had gone into it. What had I solved? The problem of my life, the riddle of my death? This is the kind of metaphysical optimism that comes occasionally as the result of too much to drink and a sleepless night. And it was all nonsense: the truth was that the simple business of swinging into action, of taking a decision, automatically gives a sense of strength and well-being. I didn't want to hear this said.

'Of course,' Mrs Hobbs said, looking out over the blue ravine, 'the best thing a woman can do is to run away. It brings the men to their senses.' She smiled suddenly, as if at some long-forgotten amusement. 'Mr Hobbs was quite a lad in his younger days,' she said sedately.

The hotel had a high, walled garden and a swimming pool. People were stretched out round its blue rim like basking seals. It was very expensive but the Hobbs refused to let me go to the cheaper hotel where Richard and I had booked.

'You are our guest, it's our pleasure, my dear,' Mr Hobbs said.

Mrs Hobbs had her picture taken beside a water-carrier. She stood there, smiling, damp with perspiration, her marrow-like breasts resting on the jutting bones of her corset. She wore a chiffon dress and walked round Marrakesh like a stately clipper, pale pink sails fluttering, stepping proudly and smiling whenever her husband looked at her, though she told me her feet were hurting. 'I've got these dreadful corns, dear, it's like walking on knives.' I took her arm and she leaned on me as if I were her daughter. Mr Hobbs beamed on us both; he enjoyed seeing us together.

I enjoyed being with them. They made me feel a young, young woman with my life before me.

We went to the hotel where Richard would expect to find me when he arrived. If he arrived. I left him a note to say where I was. 'Now you've got nothing to worry about, you can relax and enjoy yourself, dear,' Mrs Hobbs said.

The next day, the heat was intense. Mrs Hobbs looked

exhausted and after lunch Mr Hobbs took her upstairs to rest. I swam in the pool, floating until my body felt like a sponge. I had meant to doze afterwards, lying in one of the long, opulent chairs, but it was too hot: even in the shade, the air burned my skin.

I went up to my room and found Mr Hobbs waiting there.

'I was watching you from our balcony,' he said, as if in explanation.

He was wearing a silk dressing-gown, a red, purple and green paisley pattern on a dark background. He had knotted a white scarf round his neck. He touched the knot for reassurance; his hand was trembling.

I had not expected this. I pretended it was merely a social visit.

'I had an absolutely marvellous swim,' I said. 'Absolutely *gorgeous*. No one else there – everyone's sleeping.'

He said nothing, just looked at me.

'It's a lovely room, isn't it? There's a gorgeous view. Goodness, I am overworking that word, aren't I?' I smiled at him stagily but he didn't smile back. 'Come and see,' I coaxed him. He looked so stricken. Petrified.

I felt a sudden, aching pity for him. I went to the window and held out my hand.

He came. He didn't touch me but stood, staring straight ahead at the 'gorgeous view', his adam's apple moving up and down as he swallowed. An old man's neck, hidden by a white silk scarf. I thought, *for heaven's sake, you stupid, silly bitch, what would it cost you? Who the bloody hell do you think you are?*

He placed his hand on the small of my back. 'I am a foolish, fond old man,' he said.

He was a stranger. I didn't even know his Christian name Mrs Hobbs had never called him anything but 'Daddy'. I could hardly call him that. The thought made me chuckle inside. I turned to him with a little lust, a little pity. He kissed me hard on the mouth.

'I've had such dreams,' he whispered shakily. But his eyes were suddenly bright and arrogant and there was nothing unsure or nervous about his next embrace. At one point I remembered Mrs Hobbs saying *Mr Hobbs has been quite a lad in his day*, and choked on a sob of laughter.

In fact the joke – if there was a joke – was on me. I was no Lady Bountiful, graciously lending my body, nor, once over the first hurdle, so to speak, did he act as if I were. Perhaps it was absurd that I should have been surprised by this, or perhaps it was only that I had laid down such rules over the years – I hated to be hurt here, touched there – that it was astonishing to find these prohibitions disregarded. And even more surprising – to myself – I did not mind that they were.

I underwent no great 'conversion'. If I realized that there were more possibilities for enjoyment in this activity than I had been aware of recently, I was still detached, still looking down upon myself, though perhaps with more pleasure and less boredom than I was accustomed to.

And I was sorry when it was over. I remember lying beside him and putting my hand on his body and wondering whether – how soon? – we might try this again. He lay with his ankles crossed, as if on a tomb.

I remembered kissing a young man – a boy, really – in an organ loft in a country church. Dust floated in the light from the clerestory windows. Not William. Before William. We had only kissed; we were both so young, but I loved him more than William, more than Richard, more than anyone. We walked out of the church into the sunny graveyard holding hands and talking about the decay of bourgeois society. We were always discussing the decay of bourgeois society. The pity of it, I thought, the *waste*. We could have walked on, through dappled sunlight, loved each other in buttercup meadows. Instead we meet occasionally and admire each other's children. I thought: it is only dreams that are real. My heart opened like a flower, blooming with beautiful sadness. I was an old woman, going into the dark.

I was a shadow, sleeping. Another shadow kissed my forehead and covered me with something cool, a sheet of water.

I lay in a boat on a dark sea, rocking. A marvellous peace, softness.

Someone was moaning. I came up to the surface like a person drowning and sank again, out of sight. I swam up again, my lungs bursting. The room was the same; heat, veiled sunlight through drifting, white curtains. A pattern of light on ceiling. I lay on the bed, covered with a sheet, alone, sleepy and aching. Immediately in front of me, the door was open.

Dimly, this suprised me. I could see the dark corridor beyond the open door and a table with a brass pot on it, full of flowers.

Someone shouted. Hardly a shout, a rising, animal sound.

I got out of bed, tottered, reached for the white bathrobe supplied to all guests in this expensive hotel. Knotting the tie, I reeled into the corridor. My head and fingers felt swollen, my legs trembled.

The Hobbs's room was opposite mine. Their door was open. It was a large room with a double bed like a barge. Sounds came from the bathroom on the far side. I stumbled across the room, grazing my toe on something.

Mr Hobbs was on his hands and knees beside the bath. The bath seemed to be full of blood. Mr Hobbs's arms were immersed to the shoulders in water streaked with blood. He reared himself backward suddenly, and Mrs Hobbs's head and chest rose out of the pink water. Her breasts fell apart.

I knelt beside him. The floor seemed to be tilting and there was bile in my mouth. I plunged my arms in; water trickled down the neck of my bathrobe. Her body was slippery; it was like trying to catch a fish. 'Now,' I cried. We heaved together and brought her up. She was like something glimpsed just under the sea, some monster, a sea-cow. A submarine, that was it. She broke surface like a submarine; her vast, wrinkled thighs frosted with suds, like spray. There was a safety razor lying on her stomach.

I let her legs sink and groped through the water for the

plug. It came out with a dull, underwater explosion. The bile came into my mouth again, and I retched into the water.

Her head lolled against her husband's shoulder. The corkscrewed ends of her permed hair soaked his paisley dressing-gown.

A small whirlpool eddied silkily as the water began to run out. I got up from my knees, groaning – an involuntary sound like a woman makes in labour. I laid a towel on the floor and knelt again. These movements were all painful. 'Get her out, lie her flat,' I said.

Blood drummed in my ears. As the last of the water drained away, I saw the razor lying on the bottom of the bath. I concentrated on lifting the lower part of her body, clutching at the blubbery mass of her buttocks. I felt a sick revulsion as my fingers slipped between them. I have this terrible fear myself, of being split apart.

Mr Hobbs was gasping. His face was the colour of dark wine. We had her balanced on the edge of the bath, she was slipping over, falling. I crouched beneath her with my arms out, like a cradle.

'*Watch her head.*'

She was lying on the crumpled towel. The walls of the room came inwards, then receded. I knew she was dead.

Mr Hobbs was crouched above her, like a Muslim, praying. Then he flung himself on top of her; for a terrible, hysterical second I thought of some necrophiliac orgy, but he was breathing into her mouth. The kiss of life, I thought. Doesn't he know she's already dead?

How did I know it?

I picked the razor out of the bath. There was no blood now, only a pinkish scum left behind.

Where was she cut? Her wrists? Her *throat*? I had seen no mark on her.

'Doctor,' he gasped, twisting an unrecognizable face sideways.

If he has murdered her, he has changed his mind. How could I

145

have thought this – and almost laughed – as I went into the bedroom? The telephone was beside the bed which wasn't a barge, but a bier. I started to sit on the bed and remembered I was soaking wet. I stood, lifting the receiver. A voice answered in French.

'Come quickly,' I said. 'Oh, *hell*. Vite. Viens vite. Madame est . . . est . . .' *Morue*, I thought. *Morue*, a cod. 'Dying,' I said. 'Morte.'

I went back to the bathroom. He was kneeling astride her, slapping her face. I could see the marks of his fingers.

'Don't – oh, don't. . . .' He looked up at me. His face was moist, like a cheese. I remembered a child on the beach. A man had held him upside down, thumping his back. Green water had run out of his mouth. Seaweed.

'We should get the water out,' I said. I pushed him off her and heaved at her side. She slipped sideways on the floor. 'Help me,' I said. My breath came sobbing. Flat on her face, head sideways, arms above her head. We had a first aid manual at home: rigid figures in one-piece bathing suits. A small black book with white lettering. I pressed down, palms flat on the twin hillocks of her back. This was a moment fixed in time: something permanent. Mrs Hobbs on the floor and myself rocking forwards and backwards like a piece of machinery. Somewhere above me, Mr Hobbs was saying something. I thought he said something about corn, but it seemed an unlikely word in the circumstances. Green corn-fields in the spring time and love on her back.

'She's dead,' he said. 'Stop it, she's dead.' He took my wrists and pulled me backwards. I stood up, my legs trembling.

He leaned against the wall of the bathroom and cried.

Chapter Nineteen

I couldn't believe this was happening. I lay on my bed in my darkened room and made periodic trips to the bathroom.

'I can't stop being sick,' I said, when the doctor came. 'Can you give me something to stop it?'

Though it was better to be sick than to think. People retreat into illness. Life is a dream; you act a minor part, laughing or groaning. You tear your hair, miming grief. What you mourn is your own death. You know you are going to die, but death is always an accident.

'She was shaving her feet,' the doctor said. He was a plump, youngish Frenchman with a smooth skin, brown, almond-shaped eyes. His English was slow and careful.

'Her feet?'

'Her . . . corns. She had corns on her toes.'

Feet bleed easily, a lot of blood, frightening. Her heart stopped. Perhaps she had cried out and no one came.

I closed my eyes tightly. This hadn't happened.

'It was a misfortune. Her husband had left her sleeping. She should not have taken a bath alone, in her condition.'

Where was Mr Hobbs supposed to have gone? He was wearing a dressing-gown. Perhaps someone would think of this.

I said, 'Mr Hobbs came to talk to me. She was resting and he couldn't sleep. He must feel terrible.' I could not imagine how he must feel. 'They were so fond of each other,' I said.

'I have given him an injection. He is sleeping now.'

He looked at me. What was he thinking? People always make assumptions. But his face was only grave and respectfully concerned: a correct expression in the face of death. Doctors are used to death. I looked at this young man sitting gravely beside my bed. His hands rested on his knees, his throat rose like a brown, polished column out of his white shirt. I felt a sudden rush of desire for him that astonished and embarrassed me. Did it show in my face? The last time I was sick, I had seen my face in the bathroom mirror: white, sweating, hair hanging in witch-locks. *Hardly tempting*, I told myself inwardly, in a gay, mocking voice. I pulled a face, foolishly grinning. He leaned towards me, frowning like an elder statesman. 'You are in a very nervous state, madame. You must try to rest.'

I longed to tell him, 'We were making love, we killed her.' Why did I want to say this? For reassurance – *it was not your fault, she would have died anyway* – or to excite him? Fear that I might say it, dried my throat. I used to have fantasies of screaming out suddenly, in the street, in church, in a crowded bus. Why? Why should I have this desire to bring things to a point, produce some kind of crack-up, some *explosion*? Is it an alternative to sex or does everyone feel it once they have stopped being young? A desire to be involved again, to feel, to make something happen.

I thought: perhaps that's why I left Richard after all. Because I don't want to give in, become an automated machine that goes on giving the same answers, performing the same functions? Or did I leave because I couldn't face Flora at breakfast? People do things for trivial reasons. Or don't do them, out of laziness. No one is responsible any more. We have all abdicated.

I thought: what shall I do now? Fly home, get a job, find somewhere to live where Aunt Kit can be with me? A kindly landlady and a pokey room in Peckham?

I thought: I could marry Mr Hobbs and be a rich man's darling. That I could think this shocked me. I twisted round and buried my face in the pillow, moaning.

Elizabeth is exhausted, she is ill, she cannot carry any more burdens.

The doctor said soothingly, 'Try to relax. You have had a sedative. It should begin to work soon.'

Chapter Twenty

'I hate to mention it,' Richard said, 'but you can't very well stay here.'

We sat at opposite ends of my small balcony. Bougainvillea climbed over the iron rail, birds sang in the cypress trees. Richard wore his one dark tropical suit. He had arrived last night and gone with Mr Hobbs to the funeral, early this morning in the French cemetery. Since I could not think Mr Hobbs would want me there, I had pretended to be ill. I think Richard thought I had behaved badly about this. He and Mr Hobbs had been the only mourners: one of the Hobbs's sons was arriving on the midday plane.

'Frankly, we can't afford it,' Richard said. It really did embarrass him to mention this: his hand shook a little as he offered me a cigarette. Richard never smoked and disapproved of my smoking but he had bought me a packet of the English brand I liked and I was touched by this thoughtfulness. 'We've spent more than we bargained for, anyway. I know you were to be their guest here, but we can hardly expect him to think of that, in the circumstances.'

'Does it cost so much?'

'Astronomical.' He pulled a face.

'Then of course I'll leave at once. I was only going to stay until you came, anyway. That's what I told them, I mean. What's he going to do?'

'Fly home, I imagine. There are a few things to sort out of course, papers to sign. Luckily they had a letter from her doctor in case she needed medical attention, that's made the formalities a good deal easier.'

Richard knows about formalities. This is the sort of crisis

he is good at. He sighed and shook his head. 'Poor devil. He's very broken up.'

My throat constricted. 'He must feel it dreadfully, that she was alone when she died.'

'It doesn't bear thinking of. It was a terrible accident.'

He looked nervously at me as if afraid to come to the end of this conversation. We had talked of nothing else: last night, when he came to the hotel and sat with me until the drugs worked and I went to sleep, and this morning, since the funeral. It seemed tasteless to discuss ourselves in the circumstances. And it was a relief not to.

I said, 'I feel so awful. If it hadn't been for me, he'd have been with her.'

'Don't start thinking that. There's always a train of things – one's always responsible for something.'

'I blame myself, though.'

I wanted to tell him the truth, but whom would it help? Only me. I thought: there is a cheap sense in which it might comfort Richard, he wouldn't feel so guilty about Flora. I could persuade myself it was right to tell him for that reason. You can persuade yourself of anything. It wouldn't be hypocrisy.

'It's pointless to blame yourself,' Richard said. 'Accidents happen. There's always someone who could have prevented them. Only they're somewhere else, cooking dinner, or sleeping, or making love . . .'

He looked unhappy. That had slipped out.

When did she wake? Had she wondered where he was and thought he might be with me? A nice, fatherly chat? She might have come to look for him, crossed the corridor, opened the door.

It was the first time I had thought of this.

Richard said, 'You don't look very bright. Perhaps you ought to stay here, it's more comfortable. I could cable the bank.'

'I'm all right. What's your hotel like? I just left a note, I didn't ask to look at the room.'

'Not bad. No air-conditioning, but clean and fairly cool. A bit of a racket at night.'

I thought: I shan't live through this. I don't want to. It would be easier to die. But I was being histrionic: this was how I would expect to feel if I had imagined a situation like this. Now that I was actually *in* it, it was really quite different. I felt horrified and guilty, but also curiously calm – nothing, certainly, like the shocked desperation I felt I ought to feel.

I said, 'Is there a lot of traffic?'

'Not really. Noisy plumbing. Other guests with active kidneys.'

'You didn't sleep then?'

'No. I didn't want to take a pill, it was too late. I couldn't risk oversleeping because of the funeral.'

'I suppose not.'

'You slept all right, though?'

'Fine.'

'Good.'

We exchanged polite smiles. Richard looked out, over the garden.

'It really is lovely here.'

'Yes.'

I saw him go white. I prayed: don't say anything. People can do that: they say nothing and time passes. When we were first married, we argued with vain, angry faces, insisting that we should be understood in the way we wanted to be. Now we don't want to understand. The truth is too shameful.

I thought: *I* didn't lock the door? Did *he*? Would he have thought of that. And then I remembered another omission.

Richard said, in a strained voice, 'Flora's not with me, by the way.'

'Isn't she?'

'I mean, she came to Marrakesh. But she's not staying at my hotel.'

'Oh.'

'I thought you'd like to know that.'

'Yes. Thank you.'

He hesitated. 'So it's up to you, then.'

'Is it?' I found that I resented this.

'Well.' He put on a mock jolly expression. 'You're the one who's walked out on me.'

'But you might be pleased I have. Are you?'

This dialogue had no meaning for me. We were fencing, making formal passes at each other.

Richard said uneasily, 'Of course everyone dreams of walking out. But there has to be something else, some definite plan. Like another person, or wanting to walk across China. I don't want to walk across China. For one thing, there's my job. Maybe it's not important, but it's what I want to go through with. As for Flora – well, as far as I'm concerned, that's history, really. If it's a matter of choosing between a middle-aged marriage and a middle-aged affair, I naturally prefer the standing arrangement.' He looked at me. 'It's not quite like that. But I don't want to blackmail you. Flora says I've done that before. She says I've treated you badly. She's very much on your side, you know.'

'That's remarkably decent of her, I must say.'

He smiled.

'It's not funny.'

'No. It was just that you sounded more normal. Look – I want to be sensible about this. There aren't very many times when you have the chance to change, to go on as you were or do something different. If you want to go on – well, that's fine by me, though it'll have to be something different too – but if you want to leave me, for God's sake work out what for and *why*. I know in a sense you've every right to leave me because of Flora, but if you do you'll be cheating won't you, using her as an excuse?'

'God Almighty! Do you think it doesn't *matter* to me?'

'I'm sorry, I put that badly. But you've thought about leaving me before haven't you? Long before you knew about Flora. It's a sort of game you've played, I don't know why – perhaps because you like to feel you've got endless choices left, that you can shake off what you've done and who you are and start again, free as air . . .'

I said furiously, 'Did it ever strike you that you might be a bloody inadequate husband?'

'Not really.'

In spite of my rage, his rueful expression made me want to laugh as I knew he hoped it would, and this mean trick – I thought it not only mean but almost *wicked* at this moment, because it seemed to show that he took nothing seriously – made me angrier still.

'So it's all my fault, is it? For God's sake, how sly and twisted can you get? You unctuous, pompous *prig*. I suppose you've really persuaded yourself you've done nothing wrong! How *typical*.'

He pulled at the skin at the side of his eye as if to suppress a tic. 'I know I'm to blame about Flora,' he said stiffly, rather as if he was proud of his nobility in admitting this. 'But no one can go on feeling guilty, it's a neurotic trap. If you stay with me, I won't see her again. But I don't want to bargain, I don't want to *win* even. Marriage isn't a duel.'

'What is it, then?'

There must be some reason, I thought. A safeguard against loneliness, death. But Mrs Hobbs had died alone.

Anger left me. I felt coldly shocked as if I had just realized that the war film on the television screen was in fact part of the news: real people, fighting and dying.

'I don't know,' Richard said. 'A lot of things one doesn't take into account, probably.'

He was watching me. 'If you like, you can stay here on your own. You can have whatever money we've got and I'll fly home. I'll tell some story to the children. Maybe it'll give you a chance to sort things out.'

'I don't want to be alone now.'

'That's only because of what's happened. You've had a frightful shock.'

I said awkwardly, 'I was glad to see you.'

'You knew I'd pick up the pieces, that's all.'

'Now you *are* blackmailing me.'

'I don't mean to. But that's what freedom means, being on your own. Though I daresay there'd have been someone else if I hadn't come. Some father figure.'

He laughed, without amusement.

I was suddenly shivering, though it was very hot. When I moved, the sweat dried cold on my skin.

I said, 'Does Mr Hobbs want to see me?'

He looked puzzled. 'Why shouldn't he? He asked how you were. I said you didn't feel well. You don't *look* well. Perhaps you ought to lie down, have a good, long sleep. I daresay it won't break us if you stay here another day.'

He stood and took my hands, hauling me up. 'Come along,' he said briskly. 'I'll put you to bed. This was a daft moment to try and thrash things out.'

I got into bed. He straightened the pillows like a nurse. I lay flat, the sheet pulled up to my chin. My eyes felt puffy.

I thought: she can't really have seen us together. She was an old woman with a bad heart. After a shock like that she wouldn't have gone back to run a bath and cut her corns. . . .

Richard was standing at the end of the bed. I said: 'What are you going to do?'

'Well.' He looked furtive. 'Flora asked me to meet her for lunch. She asked you too, as a matter of fact, but I said I didn't think you'd want to.'

'No.'

'It wasn't a definite arrangement. I said I'd let her know. D'you mind? Because if you do, I won't go. The only thing is, I feel a bit guilty dropping her just like that. She's on her own here and it's really my fault she's here at all. She really wanted to stay a few more days, but there wasn't a car to hire or a suitable bus. She was really a bit fed up when I insisted on hareing after you. . . .' He grinned, crinkling up his eyes. 'It would only be *lunch*, I promise you that. But if you really feel strongly about it . . .'

I thought this was a pretty fair example of his disingenuous method: reducing in advance any objections I might have to a trivial level on which they seemed merely unkind or 'making a fuss about nothing'. But I felt, all at once, too apathetic to point this out to him, or even to feel indignant inwardly. Mrs Hobbs was dead: beside that, everything seemed unimportant.

'I don't feel strongly about anything at the moment,' I said, 'I only want to sleep.'

And I closed my eyes, but not before I had seen a fleeting look of triumph on his face and realized that he was quite sure he had won, that I wouldn't leave him, and that in a few days we would fly home together and everything would go on as it had done before.

Chapter Twenty-One

Mr Hobbs said, 'We were often very happy, that's what I try to remember.'

The hotel lounge was dark and cool. Glass cabinets, lit from within, displayed antique silver jewellery, the property of the dead.

We sat in our chairs like castaways. Mr Hobbs's son, a tall man with a ginger beard, poured tea.

I thought of a joke Tom and Oliver used to laugh at. Thousands of years in the future, an archaeologist lecturing, 'There used to be a curious fertility rite among these people. They used to sit in a circle round a pot that contained some kind of hot beverage – an infusion of some kind of leaf seems likely – and play this fertility game called *Now who shall be Mother?*' I wanted to laugh, not at the joke, but remembering my sons' pleasure in it.

Mr Hobbs's son had a pink, young face with a damp mouth glistening in the thicket of beard. He was gentle and attentive to his father, listening respectfully while he rambled and talking to me quietly when Mr Hobbs seemed to forget our presence and sat, staring into space.

There was no point in this meeting. I had steeled myself to comfort him, to blame myself for what we had done, but now this intention seemed not only clumsy but the most shocking presumption. What mattered was his wife's death, not his guilt, or mine. We met, not as shameful conspirators, but as strangers. He spoke once or twice about his wife; most of the time he sat hunched in his chair and let his tea get cold. I felt half asleep, sitting in this dim, tomb-like place, a cup of tea in my hand.

Mr Hobbs got up and walked away. We watched him cross the lounge and go up the wide stairs.

His son said apologetically, 'This is dreadful for him.'

'Yes.'

'Of course, we knew it might happen any time. But it doesn't come as any less of a shock.'

'Of course not.'

'At least they'd been happy. That's something to think about. Though I suppose it makes it harder for him now.' He looked at me shyly. 'D'you know, I simply can't imagine what it must be like. I tried to think, all the way in the plane. I've been married six years, if my wife died now it would be like – oh, I don't know – being split in half or paralysed down one side.' He gave a nervous little cough that reminded me of his father. 'You know, it was a mercy for him you were there,' said this nice young man. 'At least he wasn't alone. But I'm afraid it was awful for you, it must have ruined your holiday.'

After that, I couldn't bear the hotel any longer. I went out into the hot afternoon and walked through the medina.

My yellow skirt bunched up in front of me as I walked. I felt like a machine walking. My mind clicked and whirred like a camera recording; thousands of tiny cogs and levers clicking and whirring; a marvellous piece of machinery.

I thought: there is no point in guilt. The only function of

156

thought is to learn how to live, not to understand oneself: that is an entertainment for philosophers. I only know what I do, not what I am. I am Richard's wife, Tom's mother. I am Chairman of this, Secretary of that, a busy woman running a household and organizing the world on the side. Perhaps I have done one or two things I am proud of, like our old people's houses – though someone else would have done them. What am I, except a list of the things I have done, the things I have felt or said? I can remember wanting this, hating that, but I have no picture of myself as an entity, wanting or hating: there is no continuing thread.

I thought: this is the hardest thing to bear.

As a girl, I was angry about social injustice. I believed: man is a political animal. It was all very simple then: abstract ideas and institutions. People are more difficult. I thought of Richard and of our sons, Tom and Oliver. They lay in their prams in the summer time, their baby hands waving like flowers. The lines on their hands, the whorls on their finger-tips, were fixed from the moment of birth. Aunt Kit has big hands, though she is a small woman. When I have bathed her, I rub cream into them, working it in round the cuticles: I am proud of the way I take care of her.

I thought: I have to think carefully, other people depend on me. I am like a maypole, revolving: they all fly out round me, on ribbons. If I let go, what will happen? I had wanted some kind of holocaust, out of boredom, perhaps, or resentment; pulling the walls down round me. I thought I would rise like a phoenix out of the rubble.

Perhaps Richard feels the same, perhaps he wanted me to find out about Flora. Perhaps this is middle age: an urge to destroy because you cannot create any longer, become someone different. Perhaps I could have chosen differently, but it is too late now.

You have to accept this, grow through defeat. But I don't want to accept, resign; only old people do that. I don't want to look in the mirror and say, well, you've not done so badly, all things considered.

I walked through narrow streets to the big square. It was just before sunset. There were lines of stalls selling carpets, eggs, vegetables, henna, mints, dates in sticky piles crawling with flies. And beyond the stalls, the jugglers, the acrobats, the snake charmers, the water sellers, the patent medicine vendors, the actors, the story tellers. A microcosm.

Round the story teller there were a few children, listening. He sat on an empty packing case. The snake charmer had a large rug laid out on the dusty ground and a lethargic snake in a battered tin bucket. A few coins lay on the rug beside the bucket but not enough, apparently, for the act to begin. The snake charmer pointed to the coins with a contemptuous gesture and walked round the circle of watchers, lashing them with his tongue. As I approached, they drew apart to let me in: a foreigner, who would pay. I threw a coin on to the rug and walked on.

The actors were the most popular. All I could see from the outside of the crowd, were their heads bobbing up, wearing masks. Everyone was laughing. This was a comic story.

The acrobats were five little boys playing leapfrog on a shabby mat. When they saw me watching, two of them stood on their heads, unsteadily. I had only a few coins left; I emptied my purse into a small brown hand, shaking my head when they gathered round, plucking at my skirt, asking for more.

On one side of the square was a small, yellow-walled hotel. There was an outside stairway leading on to the roof. I went up the stair and stood by the parapet, looking down on the square. It was cool up here in the light evening breeze, and very peaceful, looking down on the colour and the movement. It was full of life but far away, like a film.

This was the famous square of Marrakesh, the *Place Djemaa el Fna*, the Place of the Living and the Dead.

I saw Richard. He was standing in the circle round the snake charmer, taking a movie film. The act was on now: the snake reared once out of its bucket and fell back, exhausted. I saw Richard look up at the sky, assessing the light, and adjust something on the camera. Then he held it to his eye and I thought I heard – though I couldn't have done, I was too far away – the whirr as he shot a few feet of film.

I watched him. He was middle-aged. He was a child and an old man. I could feel the connexion like a heart beat; I felt, suddenly, as if I knew the answer to everything. It was a little like being drunk. I knew it would pass, like drunkenness, but while it lasted it was a good feeling, a strange, dissolving happiness as if I could laugh at everything, and, at the same time dreadfully sad, as if I was saying good-bye to my youth. But this sadness was like a drunkard's weeping, half for the pleasure of it.

Richard took five reels of film in Morocco. He has spent nearly a year editing and titling them. Now, in the summer of the following year, we draw the curtains against the evening light and bore our friends with our holiday film. Since I have seen it so often, I am relieved when the baby cries and I have an excuse to go out of the room. She lies in the nursery, yelling blue murder because she has the sun in her eyes. Tom, working in his room, has got there before me; he picks her out of her crib and rocks her, crooning a lullaby. Against her new, petal skin, his looks old already, like leather. She is quiet while he holds her, but once back in her cot she kicks and screams and goes dark in the face, an old, old face like a wrinkled plum. Mr Hobbs's daughter, her red legs stiff with screaming.

Perhaps I can't be absolutely certain of this and perhaps it is better not to be certain: honesty is often the easiest policy, but not always the best, and Richard loves her. Sometimes it seems strange that she will never know her father but it is surprising how seldom I think of this, and perhaps even more surprising – for a woman like me, introspective, used to facing up to moral issues – that when I do think of it, it makes me laugh.

If I feel tougher now, when I laugh, perhaps that is an

illusion. I am only a year older; people don't change. The only strength is to know this, to feel yourself stretching forwards and backwards. It is a feeling, not a philosophy.

Richard would say this was a very feminine approach, to assess life in terms of feeling and personality. I would have thought it wasn't particularly feminine, only human: life, after all, is a personal matter.

This happened to me. That's all you can ever say.